In the Midnight Hour

T.B Lewis

In the Midnight Hour
T.B Lewis

In the Midnight Hour has been Copyright ©
July, 2018 Tarnita Lewis

ISBN: 978-1723265310

Adnileb Publishing LLC. Belinda Hunter CEO
hunter.belinda99@gmail.com

Acknowledgements:

I would first like to give a Hallelujah praise and thanks to The Father, Son and Holy Spirit for keeping me even when I did not think I would make it through the test. Thank you God for sending your angels to encamp around me when I was feeling weak but giving up was not an option. Thank you for showing me that through writing there was healing.

I would like to thank my family and friends who encouraged me as I wrote "In the Midnight Hour." Thanks for your encouraging words when I wanted to stop.

Thanks to my loving and compassionate husband who has rooted me on from day one and encouraged my dream of becoming a published author. You held my hand through it all and pushed me through it all. You make me feel that there is nothing that I can't accomplish. I thank you for that.

I would like to thank my world, the reasons why I push so hard, my heartbeats... my sons. Thank you for making being your mother so easy.

Thank you to my publisher Author Belinda Hunter of Adnileb Publishing LLC. For mentoring and keeping me encouraged. Thank you for all of the work and dedication you put into this book and being there to encourage me when I was in doubt. For any publishing needs please contact her at hunter.belinda99@gmail.com. She is phenomenal!

In the Midnight Hour

T.B Lewis

Chapter 1
It's A Lie

"Hello Mr. Salter," I said greeting my latest patient. "How is everything going?" Before he could reply, Mrs. Salter snarled, "He said he was fine until I had to make him come over here to the hospital." Mr. Salter had just been admitted to the Chest Pain Evaluation Unit at our local hospital. Looking directly at him I asked, "Why are you here?" He replied, "She'll tell you." In an instant, I knew both their relationship and personalities. Mr. Salter was a quiet distinguished gentleman. Tall and lean with light brown eyes. Mrs. Salter was a chunky woman standing about five feet with a beautiful head of hair and newly manicured French tip nails. I could tell she took care of herself but ate a little too much. She was definitely the type of woman who turned heads in her younger years and maybe a few at this point in her life.

Today, she forced her husband of 43 years to come to the hospital because of an episode he'd had earlier that morning on the way to his cousin's funeral. Apparently, he'd went into a deep sleep while driving and ran off the road. "I had to knock the crap out of him before he woke up," Mrs. Salter said. "He didn't want to call 911. He told me the only problem was he didn't get enough sleep last night. I asked him why didn't he come in my room and wake me up. I would have kept him company until he went back to sleep." He looked over at Mrs. Salter

with a smile which was about to turn into laughter and said, "Woman you know

you snore too loud for me." She rolled her eyes at him and continued talking.

"After the funeral he said he was fine, so we went to Red Lobster. When we got

home, that's when he started saying he was having a hard time breathing and

wanted to come to the emergency room."

"This is going to be an interesting night," I thought to myself. "This couple is

what I hope Larry and I will be in 30 years." As I listened to Mr. Salter's heart, it

sounded fine. His lungs were clear. I put on telemetry one lead at time. I then

asked questions about his past medical history. "I've always been healthy as a

horse," he said. Suddenly, a deep and raspy gasp came out of him. White frothy

foam poured out of his mouth. His arms and legs started shaking violently as his

eyes rolled back deep into his head. "He has to be seizing," I thought to myself.

Earlier, when I read his profile, he had no history of seizures. Looking at his chest,

I could see it wasn't rising and falling. I feel for a pulse. Nothing. I then pulled the

code button. I called upstairs to our sister unit to alert them that we need them

NOW. A patient has gone BAD. I placed the ambu bag over Mr. Salter's face to provide the breaths needed to save his life. His chest began to rise and fall so perfectly that the second breath went in like clockwork.

By this time, a team of nurses and doctors are surrounding his bed in an effort to save his life. We begin doing what we do best. Sure, there is lots of screaming and hollering but it's organized. We're used to it. Everyone is on one accord. I began pressing his chest up and down, up and down. In my thoughts I kept hearing someone saying, *"Live, Mr. Salter live...for the love of God live!"* I don't know where it came from but that voice was familiar. In fact, those were the same words I had to tell myself over and over again. *"Live, Tammy...for the love of God live!"* That's my name...Tammy Larson, RN. I work at a major hospital in the city of Georgetown, South Carolina. Every single day I live in my past. It makes me better at what I do.

"Epinephrine...1mg stat." The nurse pushes it. Everybody is advised to step away from the bed. All I'm hearing is "All clear...all clear." I feel my hands rise above my head. A shock is delivered. The patient opens his eyes and asks, "Where am I?" The doctor ignores him and commands, "Transfer him to CCU." The bed, the monitors and IV's move at lightning speed through the double doors leading outside the unit. The room is completely empty. Just me and Mrs. Salter are standing there. I walk up to her. She takes a deep breath...almost a wheeze then

inquires in a quiet voice, "Where are they taking him?" The fountain of tears

starts to flow. I put my arms around her and looked directly in her eyes. Without

saying a word I told her to trust me...I got you. My arms automatically squeeze as

I tell her, "I'm going to take you to a waiting room to sit while they continue to

work on your husband." As we walked arm and arm, I kept wondering why

couldn't somebody...anybody have worked that hard to save my young ailing

heart. As I was walking back into the unit, I realized I only had 10 minutes to

finish charting on Mr. Salter. But at that moment I couldn't. Because at that

moment... my own soul needed a break.

Chapter 2
The Promise to Protect Children and Fools

As I walked into the nursing lounge to calm myself with a candy bar, I smelled my grandma's biscuits. Why would I want to go back now? I asked myself. I grabbed my head. My arms started shaking. There I was back in a place when this world made sense. Like it was yesterday, I smelled the biscuits and heard my grandma musically asking, "Is Mona and Debra eating?" Neither Mona nor Debra would say a word. Debra would twist her medium length ponytails and Mona would drop her head in a shy manner. Being the most outspoken of the three; I would speak up, "We all want to eat or we will have to smell somebody's feet." We would all run to the bathroom to wash our hands and race to the small kitchen table. We knew instinctively not to go to the dining room. None of us had a care in the world as we ate a piece of Heaven on Earth wrapped up in a biscuit.

At nine-years-old, I had a confidence that was not of arrogance but one of knowing I was loved. I knew I meant the world to a number of people. The people that I knew loved me the most were my grandmother Mary Ann Bailey and my grandfather Jimmy Bailey. They were best known as Ma and Pa. My Pa was a dark skinned man with a deep voice that reminded me of a rust covered ax hitting a tree stump. Most people had a fear of Pa. He was known for pulling out his shotgun with no reservations about using it. Ma was a light skinned and very shapely beauty who was known in our small community as a woman that always tried to do what was right and just. She didn't have to put forth much effort in being angelic, it just came naturally.

I never really felt Ma and Pa were in love with each other. It was more like they owned one another and needed the adrenaline surge that came with saying, "We are man and wife." It was the safeness of for better or worse that probably united them the most. Their union produced Jackie, the woman who birthed me. Jackie was a product of the physical and mental war that constantly raged between my grandparents. I was told she was a ball of fire from birth that nothing or no one could extinguish. Nothing seemed to neither terrify Jackie nor penetrate her soul. That's why she had little ability to nurture me and my brother Dexter Alexander Clinkscale III, who arrived 10 years after my birth. Most of the time, she expected me and the people around her to do the nurturing. Jackie didn't have time for it.

Jackie loved having a good time. And everybody knew if they were with her and in her good graces they were going to have a good time as well. Jackie and my aunt Lisa, her baby sister, owned a green and brown single-wide trailer which was parked in the back of Ma and Pa's home. I often wondered why the trailer was never secured or underpinned. It stayed on wheels the whole time it was there. I guess they knew that trailer was for but a moment and not the stopping point for their lives – especially Jackie. Actually, compared to a lot of the shotgun houses in the community, that trailer was luxury.

Oh! What a place. Maylor was a small community consisting of two streets and a main road. The main road housed the black families for the first mile then the white families for the next mile. Even though we lived in such close proximity, we lived separate but peaceful lives. As the old folks would say, "We all knew our places."

From Friday night to sunset on Sunday the trailer would be packed with men and women listening to music, dancing, laughing and playing cards. Whatever high that was desired could be had from liquor to horse as long as you conducted yourself according to your choices. We children stayed on the outside making mud pies, taking turns riding bikes and swinging on the tire or swing set.

We knew going into the trailer was off limits. We would drink water from the hose pipe, do our business outside and use the leaves to wipe unless one of the grownups gave us a roll of tissue. For snacks we would eat plums, strawberries, apples, muscadines or whichever fruit was in season. We knew where to get them and sometimes we would bring the adults some back just to see what was going on in the trailer or to request a song we wanted to dance to outside. Laughter would ring out like church bells followed by some of the liveliest conversations and debates you ever heard. We all had a good time...the men, women and children.

Once dusk would set in on Sunday evening, Pa would drive up at top speed raising Holy Hell. His first stop would be his bedroom closet where he would get his double barreled shotgun and go to the back porch which faced the trailer, shoot up in the air and continue cussing like a sailor on steroids. He would keep this up until all the men were gone, all the women were in the house and the music had stopped. The only male that would take his time going to his car was Smoothe, my biological father. He and my Pa had a number of confrontations. Rumor has it that once he and Smoothe had a shootout and Smoothe shot him in his rifle hand. Pa did have the scars to prove it. In addition, Jackie shot him in the

Dexter," Jakie replied. "And look at the ring he bought me. It cost over $5,000.

And once we move to New York and make money like you wouldn't believe

hell...$5,000 won't mean anything to me."

She continued to talk as she as she packed the lime green Samsonite

suitcase and olive green night case. She didn't say a word to me nor did I say

anything to her. She and Lisa went to the front of the trailer to have a

conversation I was not privy to and then she just left. I heard the door slam so I

looked out the window. I saw her putting the suitcases into the beige car and

going through Ma and Pa's back door. A few minutes later I heard the car backing

out of the driveway and *"Midnight Train to Georgia" fading* out. Aunt Lisa came

back into the room, put some money into her top dresser drawer up under the

bouquet and mumbled. "$500 is a lot of money but I hope I don't have to use it

bailing her out." Then she continued fixing my hair.

Chapter 3
Small Town, Big City

It was the summer of 1975. I was an upcoming fifth grader. I remember my grandparents telling me, "Jackie wants you to come to New York for the summer." I immediately went into pout mode and screamed, "WHY!?" Ma said, "If we don't let you go, she would take you from us forever." Ma tried to reassure me that I would be just fine up there because she would be praying for me the entire time and we all knew the power of prayer. Riding a plane for the first time and spending time with Jackie alone was a terrifying thought for me. My mind wandered. Luckily, Susan McNeil (Susie) and her mother Susan Ann McNeil, better known as San, would be riding the plane with me. Susie was going to New York to spend the summer with her father and San was going to spend time with Jackie.

San and Jackie grew up together. They were cut from the same cloth. They were good time girls at all costs and didn't care who knew it. It's probably why Susie and I had a bond. She always introduced me as her little sister. We were both only children growing up with mothers sharing similar personalities. We knew what it was to sit in a corner and watch them party. I eventually became OK with the idea of going to New York. Boarding the plane was not at all as bad as I had expected. I had a preconceived notion that all planes were like the cargo planes I had seen on M.A.S.H. and Hogan's Heroes. Susie had flown a thousand times because she visited her daddy every summer. She tried to explain airplane etiquette to me but I just couldn't understand it until I experienced it.

The plane ride was a little bumpy but I made it through with Susie's reassurance and San allowing me to sit between them. In fact, it was a great experience. Soon, we landed at LaGuardia Airport. Jackie was at the gate to pick us up. She hugged me. I wondered what that was about but went along with it. I mean, it's not like she was the emotional type. I just couldn't put my finger on it. Later on that evening, we arrived at the apartment in the Bronx. Susie went on to her father's house. San and my mother were enjoying each other and New York with no cares or worries. So there I was in this strange new city where I was introduced to Spanish-speaking people who were both black and white. It was in the Bronx that i first learned to Double Dutch. I even learned to catch the subway. And I also learned, as a favor to my mother, how to cook up Angel Dust.

The toxic smell of Angel Dust reeked from the kitchen. It was similar to green alcohol mixed with bleach but much stronger. Most of the times when I would go into the kitchen; Dexter would be pouring liquid from this dark brown container that resembled a moonshine bottle, over something that looked like dried leaves. Then, he would bake it in a stove smaller than the ones we had at home. After baking the stuff, he would then place it in two-inch manila envelopes and stamp RED DEVIL on the outside. He would then put the packages into shoe boxes. Watching him was like observing Ma bake her cakes or kneading her dough for biscuits.

Around noon every day, except on Sunday, young fellows that looked no older than 12 would come by the apartment and pick up the product. I'm sure they were older than that because Dexter had some weird sense of moral obligation for young boys to do right and get their education. He would spend time with them. His thing was to take the young boys to the local swimming pool. He wouldn't be doing that type of business with someone so young. Anyway, as they knocked on the door, Dexter would collect the money before letting them in. Then, he would count and secure the money with a red rubber band. He would then give them the shoe boxes. Afterwards, he would joke around with the guys about the latest happenings on the block. The block was our home away from home. It was on 116th Street between Lenox and 7th. It was also a place where anything illegal or immoral could and did take place. Yet to the people who hung there, it was business as usual.

Dexter would leave immediately after the last pick up. After he would leave the house, Jackie and I would leave and head to Delancey Street with a pocket full of money. The only time I'd seen cash like that was when I would ride with Smoothe to gamble and his money didn't compare. My mouth would fall open in shock at all the things she would buy me which included anything I wanted to eat and wear. One day we were out on one of these shopping sprees when she announced she was going to have a baby. My first thought was she was having her own baby so I would get to go back to Ma and Pa. I was ecstatic because I longed to go back to Maylor.

Soon, Jackie was vomiting everywhere. She couldn't come out of the back room. She and Dexter began arguing more and more daily. He started calling her bitches from the time we woke up till the time we went to bed. In return she called him fat motherfuckers. I became so nervous and desperately wanted to escape. I would spend as much time as Ii could with the people outside as they taught me to speak Spanish and Double Dutch.

One morning, I heard Dexter telling Jackie he was losing money and if she didn't get out of the bed and start cooking up the supply then somebody else was going to start supplying his runners with dust. I heard her say, "Fuck it...Show Tammy." That's when I was sacrificed up. Dexter immediately put me to work. It became my job every morning to open the tea boxes, place them into the aluminum pans, pour the PCP onto the tea and bake up the product. Then I would fill the small yellow envelopes with the loud smelling Angel Dust and before I would stamp the manila envelopes with the words "Red Devil." I didn't have a specific time to have it ready but noon was my goal because I wanted to either go Double Dutch or go up the street to Raheim and Cassie Mae's apartment because she would always offer to cook me breakfast.

As soon as I would enter the door Cassie would comment on the smell in my clothes and on me. She would say with her hands on her hips and a frown on her face, "That smell doesn't make you sick?" I would respond, "No, but it makes Jackie sick." She would shake her head and go towards the kitchen saying in a low voice, "Come eat some breakfast." To this day I don't know if Cassie was cooking to feed her family or because she knew that at nine-years-old I was responsible for my own breakfast in an unfamiliar city.

Cassie and Raheim were from Maylor as well. Raheim was a hustler with no boundaries. His only rule was family first. Even before we ended up on the same block in the Bronx he considered me family. His mother and sisters would babysit me while my grandparents worked. Cassie was the nurturing type that believed in being a wife and mother. She didn't have a problem cooking and cleaning. She always made sure her five-year-old son was spit shined.

One hot July night, Cassie came running into the apartment in an uproar. She said she was on her way to the block. Someone had just broken into Raheim's apartment and robbed them, taking their stash money and kidnapping her baby boy Maze. Dexter told Cassie to stay put at our place and a couple of his runners were going to get Raheim.

It was no time before Raheim was at the apartment. Cassie was screaming and hollering and her tears were everywhere. She said in a very demanding voice, "I have told you over and over again this is not the life for us. I am pregnant and someone has kidnapped my son. I know one thing; you better go get him back. Raheim you better make this right." Rather than answer Cassie, Raheim pulled two guns out of nowhere. I was in a corner watching every move. Memphis, a short light-skinned man who stood 5'2" pulled out a rifle and another gun. He said, "Let's go Rah. I know where this is coming from. Word on the block was that Shorty Willis and them was gonna hit you up because they lost that two grand in that card game last week. I thought they were just talking shit." Raheim wiped the sweat from his brow and told Cassie, "I'll be back within a hour with Maze and them motherfuckers will regret the day they were born."

I tried to stay up because little Maze was like a brother to me. When I woke up the next morning, he was lying on the couch next to me without a scratch on him. I could hear Raheim and Cassie arguing in the kitchen. "You never have to worry about this happening again", pleaded Raheim. "I know I won't have to worry about it happening again because I have called my sisters and me and my kids are getting out of here. Neither my baby boy nor the child I am carrying deserves this life," she repeatedly said while hysterically crying. In one week, Cassie and the kids were gone.

I missed Cassie but I had been upgraded to hanging down on the block. After I had finished bagging the product, I would go to 116th street with Raheim or Dexter. I loved it. I saw people from Georgetown that used to hang at the trailer. I got to know the watermelon man and the women who ran the soul food

24

restaurants on both ends of the block. They appreciated such a young girl loving to eat like I did or it might have been the $20 tips I left.

Summer had ended. It was time to return to Ma and Pa. Jackie informed me that Susie and I would be flying home by ourselves. I didn't mind because the flight up to New York and the one we took to Disneyland wasn't bad at all. The only complaint about the trip to Disneyland was the way Dexter bent my fingers back for putting my feet up under his seat when he drove and the repeated instructions regarding how to empty the package of cocaine in the cup of water that was in front of me if the police pulled us over.

The night before we were to leave Jackie and Dexter got into a major confrontation. "You weren't shit before I met you. The only thing you were and still are is a dumb ass whore!" Dexter hollered with a laugh in his voice and left the apartment. For the first time, I saw Jackie defeated by another human being. She would go from furious to crying as she lay on the bed covered in white ivory satin sheets. I went and laid beside her placing my hand on her back as though I was her mother. I asked in a voice replicating Ma's angelic tone, "Are we going home?" She didn't respond immediately but after a few deep breaths and in a deep baritone voice she said," We have to get out of here but we are not leaving empty handed." I didn't know what that meant but I knew to be on guard for anything.

The next morning I noticed Dexter was not at the apartment. Jackie got up getting dressed quickly telling me to do so as well. She started piling money in our suitcases. She then packed all the clothes we had in a black trunk. She then taped what looked like a Ziploc bag full of flour to my back. At least I assumed it was flour. She instructed me to be careful with the package because it was a surprise cake batter for Ma. Just as I had thought; I couldn't wait to give Ma her special cake batter. We then caught a cab to pick up Susie. Once in the cab, Jackie taped another bag of the *flour* to Susie's back.

We didn't take the plane as scheduled. We rode the Greyhound Bus to Georgetown. I was confused but knew to be quiet and go along with plan. Once we got on the bus I whispered to Susie, "Do you know why we taking the bus?" Susie looked at me with such confidence when she said, "The bus is faster. Didn't you know? Sit up right so you want mess up the flour." I believed her and did as commanded. Although I couldn't help but think to myself that I had taken both the plane and bus numerous times and it always seemed that bus rides were longer; but what did I know. Jackie sat on the seats across from us not saying a word but I noticed the occasional tear rolling down her face.

Soon enough, we arrived in Georgetown and there was Aunt Lisa in her blue Fiat. Jackie took me and Susie into the bathroom individually to remove the cake mix from our backs. "Can I give mine to Ma?" I asked. "I want forget...I promise." Jackie completely ignored me and continued removing the tape and white powder. When we got to the car, Jackie said to Lisa "I'm going to ride a in a cab with the dope and money. You just take the kids home."

I was in paradise as soon as I saw the green and white house with smoke coming from the chimney. I could not wait to get into my Grandmother's arms. I knew the routine well. We would read a chapter out of the Bible, say our prayers and cuddle until we both fell asleep while Pa slept in his twin bed beside us.

The next day Dexter showed up and begged Jackie to come back home. Jackie refused and said that she was staying in Georgetown. Finally, she was standing her ground and refusing to put up with all of the abuse towards her and me, I thought to myself. After a few days of him begging and Jackie refusing to break he came to a compromise that he would fix up the Clinkscale house and we would make that our Georgetown home. The Clinkscale house was a house that belonged to Dexter's family but had been unoccupied for years. Jackie finally gave in and told him that she would move into the house with him once he had it remodeled. I was just happy that we were staying in Georgetown so I could be close to Pa and Ma.

Chapter 4
A Real Baby

On January 23, 1976, my baby brother Dexter Alexander Clinkscale III was

born. Since no one under 18 was allowed to come into the hospital until the day

before the discharge, I anxiously waited an entire three days before I could see

him. While I waited, Pa and I stayed at the Clinkscale house because it was closer

to my school. When I was finally allowed to see my brother, I was surprised to see

Smoothe was already at the hospital. I had not seen him in over a year. Little did I

know he wasn't there to celebrate little Dexter's birth but to welcome into the

world his own child from another woman. This meant he now had eight children

and six baby mamas. Obviously, it was confusing to me to have two brothers at

one time that weren't twins. But eventually I came to understand Jackie and

Dexter had had one baby while Smoothe and his other woman had another.

Smoothe brought roses to Jackie and her husband to celebrate their new arrival.

As time passed, Dexter's birth allowed Smoothe and Jackie to make peace of their

past hurts and become friends.

I had never had to share my maternal aunts, uncle, grandparents or even my great-grandma with anyone. And I wasn't sure I wanted to start at that point. After my initial excitement waned, my next thought was to kill my new brother. Then, one night to my surprise, Jackie woke me up and handed me little Dexter who was only six weeks old. "You are going to have to help me with him," she said. And with that, it became my job to help take care of my permanent baby doll.

For the next year, we stayed at the Clinkscale house. By this time, it had become routine to see Jackie flying to New York on a random but frequent basis. One day, I was informed that I was to be transferred to a private Catholic school downtown at Dexter's recommendation. He felt Catholic schools provided the best education. All was well until that one day when Dexter whipped me because I walked in on him and Jackie having sex. I called Pa and he was livid! He came in the house with his shotgun and told Dexter that he was not my father and to never touch me again. After this confrontation, Pa was not allowed back at the house. Because of the conflict with Pa my relationship with Dexter became strained. He became angry and no longer allowed my grandparents to babysit us. Instead, he hired babysitters to watch us. That worked out OK until they'd get greedy and steal money or start using some of the drugs left lying around. Who could blame them? It was an open feast. Nothing was put away or locked up securely. Dexter just demanded a weekly log of what was being spent. Even the thought of losing their lives wasn't enough to stop them from taking whatever they could get their hands on. There was money in the trash beneath the trash bags, in cereal boxes and in the top dresser drawer. The money lay in plain sight on top of the dresser for the sitters to take care of us. I guess the resistance to not take the money was just too much for a person who had always lived in poverty.

There was one guy named General that did quick errands for Jackie. General and Dexter's nephew were friends. Since his nephew was always disobeying rules, he was soon sent back to his mother in Detroit. Dexter and Jackie felt his disobedience might bring unwanted attention to their business. General was an overweight, dark complexioned 16-year-old who always said he couldn't read or write but could drive. So that's what he did. He drove and ran errands for Jackie and also reported any suspicious activity to her. That's how most of the babysitters got caught with their hands in the cookie jar. The punishments given out for disloyalty were so humiliating or life-altering that they never showed their faces again.

I remember one of my favorite sitters. His name was Salty. I didn't know his real name but he brought a real comfort to the home. He made sure my hair and clothes were clean and pressed. My hair was always done because he would have General take me to the beauty parlor up the street every week or two to get my hair pressed and curled. The opposite weeks he would get his done. I would hear some of the people that would visit call him a fag. I never knew the word fag was an insult. I thought it was a compliment because all I knew was he was so good to me. One day I told him what people were saying. His head dropped for a second and then he looked up and said, "I'm more woman than they will ever be." With that, he smiled and kept cooking. I noticed Dexter's younger brother Desmond would always make Salty laugh when he'd come over. Most women that came through the house were attracted to Desmond. But Desmond was in love with cocaine and heroin which were addictions he battled until the day he died.

Salty would allow me to take care of little Dexter as much as I wanted. I would change diapers, clean bottles, fix milk, wash him and all the things needed to take care of my little baby doll. Salty was good about watching me and correcting me when I was wrong in the baby's care. On one particular night, I recall being awakened by a lot of noise coming from the kitchen. Noise wasn't really unusual but I kept hearing Salty scream out, "HELP!" I walked into the kitchen. Salty turned towards me and said, "Tam... go back to bed." I smelled something foul so I went closer. I looked at the plate in front of Salty. It was covered with feces and there was a spoon on the side of it. Salty kept saying, "I gave your brother some money for his drug habit and my mama money to keep her lights on!" Jackie said with pity in her voice, "You should have told somebody, Salty." With that, Jackie got up and went to bed. Dexter and two of his cronies sat laughing. Salty looked at me again with tears running down his face and said in a deep voice that I had never heard, "Tam go to bed and be sure to pray for me." I looked in his eyes and said, "OK." As I walked out, I heard Dexter saying, "You should've been praying before you took my money!"

The next morning I went to find Salty to do my hair and help me pick out my clothes for school. He was nowhere to be found. He never showed his face again during the time we stayed at the Clinkscale house. Years later, after my graduation from nursing school, I stopped by Church's Chicken to get a bite before heading to work...and there was Salty! Something in my spirit released a worry. I don't think he recognized me as he took my order...either that or he was too scared to acknowledge me because he went to the back and never came back out. I wanted so bad to ask somebody to go get him. But something in my gut said

let it go...save him the embarrassment.

Chapter 5
He Understands Me

I went back to live with Ma and Pa for my seventh and eighth grade years. The stipulation was I had to attend St. Mary's Catholic school and spend summers with Jackie and Dexter in Harlem. I didn't get to spend as much time with my friends Mona and Debra as I would have liked, but on weekends we had adventures.

We played basketball. We took Pa's cans and bottles and sold them to the candy man and blamed it on the children up the street. We rode our bikes to other neighborhoods with a gang of three boys that were about the same age as us. Somehow, we would end up on the ball field kissing the same boys until dusk fell. Then, home we would go.

I was so glad to have graduated from St. Mary's. Maybe now, the "big feet" and "big nose" taunting I'd endured would stop. I thought I would get to go back to school with Mona and Debra. But Jackie had other plans. She said her gift to me was that I'd come and live with her in Harlem and attend a private school downtown Manhattan. In addition, I would attend modeling/charm school for the summer before classes started. Her rationale for charm school was that I couldn't eat food with a biscuit like I always did at Ma's house in the places we would be traveling. I thought, *"Why not? It's good that way."*

Jackie allowed me to have a sleepover at the Clinkscale house to say goodbye to my friends. Everybody I invited came except Susie. She was moving in a different direction at that time. She had quit school and she and her mama San had started competing over men. I didn't understand her quitting school because she was the smartest person I knew. She had tutored all of us at one time or another and was the first African-American cheerleader at the local high school. "She has it all," I always thought to myself. When I would tell her, "You are so beautiful and smart. You are going to be a doctor or lawyer." She would always respond with, "What looks good is not always good." I loved her to the day she was killed at aged 33 in a tragic car accident. Rumor was none of her remaining family had money to send for her body. So the State ended up cremating and burying her in a pauper's grave. At my going away party Debra, Mona, Nancy, Sandra and I had a good time. Even though fighting was not our forte, we always got into one at the pool near the Clinkscale house. My Aunt Lisa dated the lifeguard but it did not stop the fights. We were constantly laughing and talking which would cause people to think we were picking on them. As soon as swim time was over we could tell by the looks we were receiving it was going to be a battle. The one thing I wished I had was Jackie's ability to fight. We knew we were in trouble as soon as we got dressed and the assistants would give our rivals the hose to wet us up. That's when I missed Susie the most. She was not afraid of a fight. She and Debra would give anybody a good butt kicking. By the time we would walk out front, the crowd would be waiting for us.

Everybody would pick a person they wanted to fight. Sandra and Mona would start walking toward the house or hiding behind the cars to keep from participating. I knew I would be first, so before I stepped up I would ball my fist up and flail my arms in a windmill motion until I wore myself out and fell down. Next was Nancy. She would hold her own but would apologize to the person after the fight – especially if she saw blood. The last of the battle would be when Debra would brutalize whoever got in her way. Once she finished, we were always free to go. The entire time we were walking back to the Clinkscale home Mona and Sandra would apologize for not fighting. Debra would cuss us out for always laughing at people causing her to have to fight in the first place.

Although we got into a fight it didn't ruin the day. By the time we got back to the Clinkscale home we had to change our clothes. Everybody took a bath while listening to music, dancing and singing until we all fell asleep in my pretty, pink bedroom. It was a room that had pink walls, pink comforter, pink carpet and a pink flowered comforter. My friends would always laugh and say it felt like sleeping in a bottle of Pepto Bismol. That was my last experience with pure friendship with no strings attached.

A couple days after my goodbye party, we were getting ready for our flight to New York when Jackie introduced me to one of Desmond's love children. His formal name was Peter Lane and he was eight- years-old. We called him Pete. It was Pete's first time meeting his father. As it was, Dexter and Jackie had a thing for taking in young men who were having a hard time in life. Pete was a product of a single mother who constantly struggled to keep the essentials in place for him and his younger brother. Desmond was not interested in getting to know his son and his mannerisms spoke volumes. He might have said hello to Pete and that was about the size of it. So Dexter decided Pete would come to New York for the summer to show him a better life and to get to know him better. Even though he was young, Pete knew how to fend for himself. We bonded instantly. Being a quick learner, he was good at helping me complete tasks appointed to me by Dexter and Jackie. The chores ranged from cutting dope and cleaning seeds out of weed to cleaning the house. The cool thing was we could do it together. Pete became my confidant. He was one of my favorite people. We had no telephone at the time, so Pete and I would talk to each other until I got enough quarters saved to call my girls in Georgetown. To be honest, there were a lot of days when Pete kept me from killing myself or losing my mind. He saw firsthand the beatings I received and heard the curses hurled my way. He would always apologize for the person assaulting me and suggest that we get little Dexter and go to the park.

Chapter 6
My Stomach Hurts

Pete left at the end of the summer. The fact that I was in school took a lot of the pressure off of me. I had hours away from the chaos. That was until Big Dex messed up a run of dope he was supposed to turn with a hustler named Bottom. The shipment was from California and turned out to be quinine. Dexter didn't do drugs at the time. And the person he was going to take to sample it went into the bathroom at the airport and OD'd and had to be rushed to the hospital. That was when the real drama began. Bottom sent threats to the house that if Dex didn't get him his $40,000 then he would pay with his life.

Dexter left New York headed for Detroit. The pressure from Bottom's intimidation had gotten to him. He didn't have the money and didn't have any resources to get it. Dust was not the popular drug anymore as heroin and cocaine had taken over. His street credibility was gone in New York. No one wanted to do business with him. Plus, Bottom was too dangerous. He was known to leave houses full of people dead. Soon, Dexter left for new territory leaving Jackie, little

Dexter, Crystal and her son Ronald and myself to hold down the fort until Bottom

came to his senses. There was a lot of tension. Jackie was receiving constant

threats. But little did Bottom and his boys know, Raheim was Crystal's brother. He

ran the pool room on the block and kept up with all the news. Raheim was

militant and had no limits in the game of hustle. He was mannerable but when it

came to business he was taking no prisoners. We knew someone had our backs so

it made a tense situation more bearable.

Crystal had an apartment in the Bronx which we used as a getaway when

things got a little too hot in Harlem. The first couple of weeks after Dex left, we

went to the Bronx apartment to lay low. Jackie and Crystal would occasionally go

to the block on 116th street to check out what was happening on the block.

Raheim told them everything was cool and that Bottom only wanted Big Dexter.

When they got back to the Bronx, they told me to pack up my stuff because we

were going back to our place in Harlem. Jackie said she was tired of driving me

back and forth to school and she had to sell some product to generate some

money because she had bills to pay. By then Crystal had a love interest on the first

floor of the Harlem apartment that was deep in the game as well and he was

nothing to play with without severe consequences.

I continued to go to school at Baldwin. I was developing friendships and starting to have a crush on one of the guys. I was instructed by Jackie and Crystal to go to school and come straight home afterwards or I would get my ass kicked. As all teenagers do, I decided to test the waters. I went to a school basketball game and to get pizza with friends afterwards. We didn't have a phone line so I couldn't call. I had at least $300 in my pocket at all times in case something jumped off with Bottom. I had the option of getting to the Bronx place, getting a hotel until things calmed down or taking a cab to the airport to get a ticket to Georgetown.

When I arrived home after the game, Jackie and Crystal were on the fire escape looking out. I could see their heads but not their facial expressions. I couldn't wait to share my experience. As I turned the key to unlock all of the locks the door flew open. I don't know which one hit me first or harder. They beat me so bad that I felt I was in a state of delirium. I thought I was still at the game. I finally regained consciousness to the sound of hoes, motherfuckers and bitches. As I lay there hurt more mentally than physically, they both explained to me the danger I'd put them and myself in by not coming home on time. Then I was told to get up, wash my face and go to the corner Chinese restaurant and get the food on the list handed to me by Jackie. Somehow, I found the strength to get up and go into the bathroom. Afraid to look in the mirror, I threw cold water on my face over and over again. It didn't burn so maybe I had no scars. So I looked and seeing no bruises or open wounds, I knew I had nothing to explain at school the next day. In a weird, grateful way I was ready to go get the food.

A couple weeks after, there was more drama. It was almost Thanksgiving. Ma and Pa were coming to spend it with us. I was so glad I was going to get some good cooking and I would get to show Ma the church I found up the street. It was around 11 pm. I was lying in the front room on one of the cots that served as couches during the day. In the room sleeping with me on separate cots were little Dexter and little Ronald. There was a loud knock at the door. Something about that knock woke me out of a deep sleep. I could feel death at that very moment. I could smell it, taste it and see it. Jackie went to the door and looked out the peephole. I had a clear view of her down the hall. She then opened the door. In stepped Alvin. Usually, I would get up and greet him because he was always very nice to me. This time something in my soul told me not to get up and keep quiet.

Alvin stood there looking disheveled and nervous. Inside I already knew. He was there to kill us. It was so strange. I began writing his name in the carpet over

42

and over again. I knew he was there for more than dope or quinine. My thought

was if his name was written in the carpet at least somebody would see it and

know who killed us. Alvin said he wanted to buy some blocks which are quinine to

cut heroin. I knew we had a closet full because I'd put them in there earlier.

Thoughts of death continued to run repeatedly through my mind. My throat

seemed to be closing up. I needed some water but something in me said, *"Don't*

move." I began praying in addition to writing his name again in the carpet with my

index finger over and over again until my palms were sweaty. I heard Jackie say,

"We're out of blocks but we are expecting a shipment in about an hour or so.

Come back then." I think he spotted the pistol Jackie had in the pocket of the blue

silk robe she was wearing. So my mind started planning as well as writing Alvin's

name in the carpet one more time. I told myself if she pulls out the gun

immediately grab the boys and get on the fire escape. Alvin grabbed the door

knob, looked back, wiped sweat from his forehead and said, "I'll be back in an

hour." When he left out and I heard the police lock close, I jumped up and

screamed out, "Jackie I could feel death!" She replied, "I felt it too." Then she got

up, went to her room and fired up a joint. I went back to the front room, laid back

on the cot and stared at the ceiling all night. Alvin came back in an hour as

promised and beat on the door for over 15 minutes or so. I didn't move nor did

Jackie. She just said in a clear confident voice after he stopped beating on the door, "That will never happen again...I promise you that will never happen again." Two days later, on Thanksgiving Day, someone walked up to Alvin and shot him in the face. It was rumored he laid on his back in the snow for a couple of hours while people walked over him.

That was devastating to me. We'd spent the last Thanksgiving with this man. He was nice and funny. Jackie just told me get over it. She even told me I did the right thing by lying there and keeping my mouth shut that night. "Word on the street," she said, "Alvin didn't know who was laying on the cots in the front room. He thought you might have been Crystal so he didn't want to take a chance on his life. Little did that motherfucker know he took a chance by not completing his job." No one talked about Alvin losing his life on the block of 116th street again. I still don't know to this day if the hit was from our team or Bottom's.

We began packing to go spend Christmas in Detroit with Dexter. I remember saying goodbye to my hanging crew at school. We all went to eat pizza then began our goodbyes with hugs and high fives. I finally got to hug Eric, the guy I had a crush on for months. He reciprocated the hug. That meant the feeling there was more than just friends. That was a grand Christmas present. The both of us knew after Christmas break we would start a relationship.

When I arrived back on my block, little did I know my life was about to change. I heard a commotion while I was walking up the stairs. It sounded like two men fighting over a woman. As I got closer, I could hear the familiar voices. When I turned the corner I saw Raheim standing with a silver gun to a man's head. I didn't recognize the man outside in the hall, nor did I recall the man Jackie had sitting on the sofa with a gun to his mouth. The only thing Jackie said to me was, "Get your bags and the money and take them to the station wagon. Crystal is getting the other things together and taking them to the van. We are in some serious shit baby girl. We have to get out of here before these motherfuckers kill us!"

I began packing money and things I deemed important. Then, I helped Crystal get the other things. We made only two trips. The whole time I felt like I was going to defecate or vomit. Crystal's boyfriend came up and took the gun from Jackie. I began throwing black trash bags in the back of the station wagon just assuming it was dope, money and clothes. It seemed like it took forever but it actually took only three or four minutes at the most. I asked Crystal where the boys were. "They in the van," she said. The neighbors sitting on the stoop ignored us just like it was just another day.

The van and the station wagon ignitions were running the whole time. On our last run it was dusk. "Big Tam this is it," Crystal said to me out of breath. "Go to the station wagon and sit in the driver's seat. We are coming right behind you. If we don't come in four minutes, get the boys and call the law." I did as instructed and headed for the station wagon. I glanced over by the cot. Mark had one of the guys flat on his stomach with his knee in his back. I knew we were safe at least from this guy because blood was flowing from the back of his head. Raheim had another guy bent over the coach with his gun in the man's mouth as he straddled him. "Hurry up!" he hollered. "Hurry up before the law gets here!"

I sat in the driver's seat waiting for the next move. My four minutes were almost up. I had my hand on the door handle when I saw Crystal and Jackie come out running to the van. Raheim came out right behind them and slid beside me in the passenger seat. "Put the car in drive, Big Tam," he ordered. "All I need you to do is drive up a couple of blocks then I will take over." The only thing I could think of was, *"I am 13 and my period is on...and I'm bleeding."* My heartbeat was so rapid! The fear was nearly paralyzing me. But as I swallowed, I put my foot on the gas. I could smell and taste the sweat. I drove the requested two blocks when Raheim told me to pull over. I hurriedly obliged. He got out and ran around to the driver's seat and I scooted over to the passenger seat. Once we got to Crystal's place in the Bronx, I must have fallen asleep or passed out. The next day, Crystal and Jackie organized the cars and we were on our way to Detroit.

The move to Michigan was not easy nor was it wanted by anyone involved. At that point, I believe Dexter was running for his life. He was more on edge and must have been on drugs. All I know is I became more of a target than usual. That is when the physical and mental abuse became almost unbearable. For example, I became known as Bruiser. I have no idea why he chose that name. But I did know I never liked it. That name did not fit who I felt I was inside which was a sensitive, caring and most of all giving individual.

We moved in with Marianne , a friend of the family, and her children. She was an ex-felon who had served many years in federal prison for a lover's dope deal that had gone badly. Marianne was now legitimate for the most part. She was now in cosmetology school and doing well. I'm assuming she let Dexter and Jackie stay at her home for the financial gain while they looked for a place of our own. That summer was good in so many ways. I got to know Donnie and Debra who were Marianne's children. That summer was filled with wonderful times as we bonded. During those days it was just Donnie, Debra, Pete, Tangy, Dexter III and me. I was always in charge at 13-years old. We were left alone for hours upon hours. We didn't mind it though. Not one bit. We danced, sang and ate. We went to eat at Big Boy's on Eight Mile every day. We would walk at least three miles to the amusement park and just enjoy ourselves. In fact, that summer, we all formed a spiritual connection that has not been broken to this day.

For some reason, Fat Dexter's resentment towards me was constant during that summer. I don't know if it was the stress of knowing he was a hunted man or the fact I was turning into a young lady before his eyes. He did the weirdest things. He would come in and announce that he was taking me shoe shopping. I had a very large foot for a girl at that time. In fact, I wore an 11 narrow. It was unheard of for a 13-year- old girl to have that size foot. Something in me kept wondering why we were taking this venture alone. We went to the Naturalizer shoe shop. Any shoe I liked, he refused to buy. According to the person assisting us, the shoes he picked out were for a person of 60 or 70 years of age. Even though the person helping us suggested I get something more age-appropriate, Dexter denied her request. He told her how much he was spending and had her bring out more of the granny shoes. He even got me a few shoes from the men's

section. Once we got back to Marianne's home, she screeched when she saw the

shoes. She offered to take them back herself and get me something else. But Fat

Dexter threatened that if any of the shoes were returned, he would take them all

back and I would go barefoot for the rest of the summer. The other stipulation

was he better see me wearing the shoes. The silence in the room let everyone

present know that it was not up for discussion.

Chapter 7
I'm in Your Hands

Dexter had an older sister named Eleanor who had a reputation for being the queen of drug transport. She was a beautiful airline stewardess. She reminded me of Lena Horne with a short meticulous haircut. She was very shapely and constantly talked about getting silicone breasts. She was even able to convince Jackie to get a set of her own which may have been the cause of Jackie's health issues that came later. Eleanor was articulate and constantly reminded people around her how educated she was because the airlines would not hire anyone without a college degree. Most people believed her because it was rare to see a black stewardess.

She would constantly call me country, ignorant, tomboyish and most of all silly bitch. But her whole attitude would change when she needed me to make a dope run with her somewhere around the country. She would dress me in some of her clothes and shoes. My toes would hang over the sandals but it didn't matter because she was sugar sweet to me while we were on the plane. When we returned from our trip, she would put back on her stripes. In her presence, I didn't

know if I would get the tiger or the bunny rabbit.

I was so glad when we moved away from her to Ann Arbor. Blossoming into

a young woman and the hormones that came with that process, I could tolerate

one Clinkscale, but not two. During that time, Jackie didn't spend much time at

the townhouse we'd moved into. Crystal moved from New York to help take care

of us because Jackie was spending more time in Georgetown. Crystal stayed until

even she could no longer take Dexter's verbal abuse. Soon, she packed her bags

and headed back to Georgetown too. Her job had rescinded their layoff.

Eleanor sent her son Gregory, who was now 17, to stay with us once again

for a couple of months. I didn't know if he and Dexter were feeding off each other

but I couldn't help but feel as though Gregory and Dexter despised the very air I

breathed. One Saturday morning Jackie was home and took me to Detroit for

Marianne to fix my hair. It was beautiful. I felt pretty even wearing the men's

loafers. When we returned home, I stood in the kitchen looking for something to

eat. I noticed that Gregory's friends were watching me. I had such low self-esteem

I thought he and his friends were mocking me instead of admiring me. I

remember Gregory hollering out, "Uncle Dex...Tammy is down here showing off for these boys. She needs to get her fast ass upstairs." I remember having a

sandwich in my hand...taking a bite...then the next thing I knew a bucket of fish

and ice water came pouring down over my head. My fingers went back as though

we were playing mercy. In an instant, I was on the floor. My hair that gave me a

little self-worth was soaked. "Get that shit up and go to your room, you stinking

bitch!" Dexter yelled. It took everything in my soul to try and get up. I was on my

knees contemplating whether to cry, curse or run fast as I could to my room. I

can't remember the reaction of the guys at the table but the only two laughing

were Dexter and Gregory.

I finally got up with tears in my eyes but stubbornness in my heart. I

refused to let out the cry of torture I felt. I looked up to heaven and refused to

give them the satisfaction. I began cleaning the mess up, putting the fish back into

the white Styrofoam cooler. I whispered to Dexter, "You need to go get some

more ice for the fish. I was still soaked and remained soaked while I cleaned

everything up. Pete, now 11, came into the kitchen and started helping me. The

crowd left immediately. No one said a word to me.

As I passed my mother's room, I could smell the marijuana coming from

beneath the door, so I knew not to stop but to continue walking to my room.

Once I crossed the threshold of my door, my knees buckled. I lay across the bed and cried from places and parts of my soul I had yet to know existed. Pete eased into the room and watched me. He began to cry as well. He reassured me none of this was my fault. In a soft reassuring voice he looked into my eyes and said, "This is no way your fault. I don't understand why Uncle Dexter and Gregory treat you so bad. I know it will get better." Somehow, I believed in him and what he said to me.

We spent two years in Ann Arbor. We would switch schools every six months because of Dexter's paranoia of people robbing us or killing him. As a teen, I didn't comprehend that because he would bring drug dealers and addicts to our home. He always had someone that would pretend to be his flunky by hanging on to his every word, constantly in agreement with him and doing every task he requested. It only took six to eight months before his flunkies found out that he was not as tough as he pretended. He needed an entourage to give him courage. They would then take from his stash or get tired of his shit talking, curse him out and threaten to kick his ass. Before I knew it we were moving again. After we would move to another side of town or in another school district, I was told not to socialize with anyone because Dexter wanted only immediate family in the house. But he never followed his own rules.

I found something that kept me away from the house. I started running track and playing basketball. Being a very tall and naturally athletic girl, I assumed that trait came from Jackie and Smoothe. They both were known athletes in Georgetown. Plus, all the time I'd spent playing sports with Mona and Debra made me pretty good. My coaches would ask where my parents were. I would always say at home or working. "What do they do for a living?" I would always say," My mother is a nurse and my stepfather is a pilot." They would then pretend they understood why they didn't make any of my track meets or basketball games. Little did they know, I signed my own permission slips. In a passing thought I would tell Jackie or Dexter, "I'm staying after school for practice for basketball or track." Sports gave me moments of normalcy. That is until one of them would forget and come to the school looking for me. I guess the staff would tell them we had practice, an away game or meet. When I would get back home, they would swear I didn't tell them I had a game or meet and threaten to make me quit the team. The excuse was my grades weren't good enough to participate in after school activities. I really knew the concern would come in when I wasn't there to cut some dope, walk a dope addict that had overdosed or find a good vein for one of the heroin attacks. The children would occasionally be the excuse but Pete had become proficient in holding them down.

I felt lucky to remain sane. My stomach was always in an uproar. In addition to a very nervous abdomen, my grades were horrible. Dexter would post my grades on the refrigerator. Everybody that came in the house was instructed to go see my grades. I was building up so much resentment and anger towards him and Jackie too for not caring for me. I would pray to God and tell Him in what order I wanted them to die. Unfortunately, that's the year Jackie was diagnosed with breast cancer. Everybody was saying it was from the silicone breast implants. I prayed hard telling God I didn't mean what I said when I'd wished they were dead. "I can take it," I prayed. I didn't want anybody to suffer. But was it too late? Weeks later, she had her right breast removed and started chemotherapy treatments. She was doing really well with her treatment as long as her marijuana was kept in good supply.

Chapter 8
Enough is Enough

May 18, 1982 was the day I decided enough was enough. That was the day

that the shit hit the proverbial fan. As usual, Big Dex woke me up taunting me

with laughter in his voice as he snickered, "Get yo' big ass up and cook breakfast!"

My immediate thought was either this muthafucka' needs to be dead or

somebody needs to take me out of my misery. That was also the day Dexter and I

got into our first fist fight. I tried to appease him by doing as he commanded and

got up to cook. I began making pancakes, bacon and cheese eggs. No requests

were made, so this was the breakfast I began preparing. Dexter dragged all of his

flabby 400 pounds into the kitchen wearing just his underwear and tilted glasses

on his face. With a mouthful of pancake, he snarled, "I announced last night

everyone in this house is cutting out all sugars and breads." Because I disobeyed

this command, he administered his usual punishment for me by bending my

fingers back. All the while he called me stupid bitch after stupid bitch. His new

flunky raised up off the couch to see what was going on because our screaming had become unbearable. "You will finish making this breakfast but you won't eat a drop!" I made up my mind once I got a feel that the mood that day was going to be foul. I wasn't taking this shit today. Not from anybody. I took the mix, the pancake batter, sausage, bacon and eggs and put them all in the garbage disposal. I walked with my head up and shoulders back to sit in the wicker chair in front of the television. Its bird cage shape somehow gave me a sense of protection. As I was walking over to the chair I was asking God why we couldn't have a phone so I could call somebody down South so this would stop. I wouldn't let Dex bend my fingers when he tried and he blew a gasket. The guy on the couch watched as though we were a soap opera. He was shaking his head the whole time. After the first confrontation was over, Dex went to the back and started smoking a joint with Jackie. I could tell by the rank smell it was laced with something.

Soon after, Jackie came into the front room. She looked down her nose at me as I sat in my secure birdcage chair and asked, "What the fuck is going on in here? You acting like you ain't got no damn sense!" I remained silent but was wishing this could all just be over. By then Pete was awake. As she berated me I thought, *"What more could they want?"* I looked her in the eye, got out the chair and turned to go to my room. *"I'm staying in there all day,"* I thought to myself.

But before I could take a step, she hit me in the shoulders with two powerful

blows. By this time everybody was up watching the circus. I screamed out to her,

"What the fuck?! Do you want me dead?" Before she could respond I said, "Fuck

it. I'll help you out and kill my own damn self." The bathroom was a straight shot.

So I ran into it and locked the door. "I will no longer be the freak and I won't shed

another tear for your fat ass, red-faced husband either." I said it low because of

fear but loud enough for them to hear me. By this time in my life I could be just as

verbally abusive as everyone else around me. I sat on the toilet not really wanting

to kill myself but thinking I had better go through with it or they will call me out as

a bullshitter. I looked around. Something inside said, "Don't give them the

satisfaction." To be honest, I remembered that somebody once told me if you

killed yourself then you would automatically go straight to hell. It must have been

Jesus himself talking to me. Jackie shook me out of my stupor by yelling just

outside the door, "Bitch if you don't come out of that bathroom I'm going to kick

your stupid ass!" She then kicked the door in. *"She really does care,"* I thought.

She stood over me in a warrior stance and canceled any thought of her caring by

beating me unmercifully with her fist. As she beat me she threatened to kill me

herself. Her grinding teeth and blood shot eyes told me she meant every word she

spoke. She told me to go put an ice pack on my face where she had hit me in the mouth as though that punch was an accident. She followed behind me to get the ice and instructed me to sit down in that wicker chair and not to move. With my soul in a thousand pieces I sat there trying to think what Ma would tell me to do? She would advise me to pray for them but I couldn't. I sat there with the Ziploc bag full of ice on my face trying not to have any thoughts. The flunky dope addict sat on the couch staring at me for hours not saying a word and only getting up occasionally to use the bathroom. His eyes and posture spoke more to me than his mouth as if to say, "I wish I could help you but this habit won't let me."

Dexter III was hyped and running around getting into everything. Pete would walk by my chair and quietly ask if I was OK. I would nod yes. He would get something out of the fridge and go back to his room with his book. I started feeling a little better as my state of despair lifted. My favorite show, *I Love Lucy* came on which gave me something to distract me enough from my worries to at least laugh. Little Dex came and sat in my lap and we continued watching television. Half way through the show he jumped off my lap as if something had happened and ran down the hall to Jackie's room. Suddenly, from my left peripheral vision, I saw a yellow blob. I turned to see what is was and this 400-pound killer whale was charging at me with a belt. "You crazy bitch!!!" Dexter screamed. Then he hit me across the chest twice. *"What had Little Dex said I'd done?"* Before he could hit me again, I surprised myself by snatching the belt away from him and turned it in my hand to where the buckle could hit him with every swing. No one rushed to stop it. Jackie might have been sleep or high but she strolled casually in the room to see Dex's glasses lying on the floor. Jackie somehow got a sense of urgency when she grabbed him and pushed me back. I fell into one of the cabinets. I immediately got up still swinging at nothing but air. I could hear the flunky saying, "She was just sitting there! She was just watching TV. She didn't do a thing to Dex! I watched her the whole time like you told me. Get me back to the city. I can't take this no more. This shit is crazy." He hung his head and walked out the door as distraught as if all that transpired had happened to him. Dexter stood there huffing and puffing because he couldn't catch his next breath. He looked at me in disbelief. Jackie was sweating and I could tell she needed either a strong drink or a joint...maybe both. She told Dex to come into the bedroom. I heard them fussing as I sat back in the wicker chair. The flunky stuck his head back into the door looking straight past me with no eye contact, "DEX!! LET'S GO! I NEED TO GET BACK TO THE CITY!" A few minutes later Dex wobbled by me with a defiant look on his face and walked out the door slamming it shut. I knew from routine Jackie wouldn't be coming back out so I could finally eat and have the run of the house. But from that point on I knew I was going to

have to watch my back if I was going to survive in this so called home.

Chapter 9
There is Good People Out There

I made it to the summer of my upcoming junior year of high school. I'd registered myself for summer school because my regular grades were crap and the only way I was going to play basketball was to pass the classes I'd messed up in. By this time, I had found a safe haven in my best friend April's family. The Mooney's were a legitimate family that worked regular jobs. Her dad was a manager at the Ford plant in Detroit. Her mom was a teacher at one of elementary schools in Ann Arbor. I would always listen as she gave April such calm sound advice on life's lessons. Mrs. Mooney always spoke in a calm voice. Any time she spoke she had my full attention. She would tell her daughter about holding on to her virginity because sexual experiences were only for husbands and wives. She'd say things like, "If something were to happen... and I'm not condoning sex before marriage...but please use protection. Know that God will protect you and regardless of what happens, always keep a sense of spirituality and educate yourself." Her lectures resound with me until this day because it reinforced the same principals Ma preached.

By this time I met April at Pioneer High school I was allowed to choose my own wardrobe. The first thing that went out the door was the men's shoes Dexter made me wear as a punishment the prior year for having bad grades and big feet. April was a shy girl that always tied a jacket around her waist. I noticed her because I wondered why she would hide such a nice figure. She and I had our first encounter in Algebra 2. The first month we didn't have much to say to each other besides hi and bye. She probably thought I was a loser because I only showed up to class one or two times weekly. I enjoyed socializing in the halls. I was having fun and I knew we would move again soon and this was the place I felt important. People enjoyed my jokes.

One day I decided to go to class. A girl named Tina came into the classroom and gave me an invitation to her birthday party. She was a popular girl and if you were invited to her party you were in the IN crowd. I looked over at April and saw the disappointment in her face. I knew disappointment oh so well. She said Tina probably forgot to give her an invite and was going to bring it later. So I invited her to be my guest at the party. She finally accepted.

It was on and popping after she said OK. I took over planning our hair appointments and what we would wear. April offered for us to get dressed in our identical outfits at her house. Just so happened, we lived in the same neighborhood and didn't know it. We practiced our dances, how we would walk and how we would talk. We planned on being the belles of the ball. The chemistry between us was so easy. We had the time of our lives with each other and became inseparable.

I was not the only person partying. Jackie gave a big party at the Renaissance to celebrate the fact she was cancer free. Even though she had been on chemo and radiation, she retained her strength and poise. She was rarely nauseated and didn't lose any of her hair. By the end of that year she was told the cancer was in remission. While planning her party, she appointed me to babysit so people could bring their kids. I was excited because April would be coming with me and we could enjoy the pool. Plus, Jackie said Smoothe my biological father was coming. April said, "Maybe you can tell him how they are treating you." I replied, "I haven't seen him in almost six years and he has eight other children. I don't know him. Who knows, he might not care."

We checked into the hotel. I was glad to see so many people from Georgetown. People were dropping their children off. After I ordered pizza for over eight children I went out into the hall to get some ice. I heard Jackie say,

"There she is right there." So I turned around. I saw a man and a woman standing with Jackie wearing a matching cowboy outfit. "Tam!!" the man loudly said and ran up to hug me. I looked into his face. It had to be Smoothe. I looked just like him. "They been taking care of you up here?" he asked me in a squeaky voice. I really wanted to scream "NO!!! TAKE ME AWAY RIGHT NOW!!" Instead, I smiled and lied. "Yeah...pretty good." "You look good," he said looking me up and down. "You are so tall. Do you play basketball?" All I could do was nod my head yes to every question.

Soon, Jackie came down the hall knocking on doors telling people the partying was about to start and a key was needed to get to the upper level. Smoothe then said, "Well, I'm going to the party. I'll see you after it's over." I nodded my head yes again. I went into the room and told April I saw my real dad. She asked me if I'd told him how badly I was being treated but I shook my head no. We didn't bother anymore with the conversation. We just began entertaining the kids.

The next morning Smoothe and his girlfriend Vera came to my room. It was just me, him, his girlfriend and April. I noticed he was still wearing that cowboy hat. He crossed his arms as he sat on the edge of the night stand. He then asked me if I was going to come visit him. I shrugged my shoulders. He then said, "I'm gonna give you a little bit of money and hopefully you can come to Georgetown." He then handed me a $100 bill. I thanked him. He hugged me again and left the room. I desperately wanted to say, "I have plenty of hundred dollar bills! Look in the night stand. I just need you to protect me!"

Big fat Dexter got a glimpse of the unity April and I shared and vowed to split us up. He would always say I was putting his business in danger by bringing people in and out of the house. So, I started hanging more at April's place. His thought process changed after Jackie went to Georgetown for about two weeks and he needed someone to watch the kids.

April and I decided to have a summer party at one of the local hotels. Dexter said he would fund it if I kept the kids for a couple days while he was in Detroit. I agreed. April and I would keep an eye on the kids for the next few days while he made a run. Then, on the weekend, we could have our party.

Just like he said Dexter fronted the money for the party. He made sure we had enough for food. He even went to purchase the liquor. The party became the talk of the neighborhood because we would be serving liquor. This party was going to be a success.

Dexter watched us load up all the food and liquor into April's mother's station wagon. He offered an ounce of weed to the guys that were helping us. Such excitement!! The guys and girls loading up kept saying this was going to be the party of the year! Dexter called me back into the house. So I went to see what he wanted. I could not believe we were getting along so well. Maybe this was the turning point in our relationship.

Then he said with a straight face "I'm taking the boys with me to Detroit... and you won't be attending that party." I leaned back, smiled and said, "You are kidding aren't you?" He said "No...how in the world are you gonna party if you can't even spell party. You know what your grades look like. Dumb bitch you better not leave this house." My mouth dropped. My only thought was Mark House was going to be at the party. He was handsome and the caption of the basketball team. And everybody was saying he liked me.

April came back in to see what was taking so long. She saw me sitting on the couch like I was out of breath. Dexter said in his usual sinister laughter, "She is not going. She needs to read a book. "April walked up to me. "What happened?" she asked. I shrugged my shoulders. With that, he grabbed little Dex by the hand

and Pete followed him out the door. "I'll go drop everything off and let everybody in the rooms then I'll come back here with you," she said calmly.

April did come back. We sat there until midnight. Finally curiosity got the best of us and we decided to go see what was going on at the party. Once we got there everyone was greeting us and asking where we had been. April said she had to work to closing and I said I had to wait for her to pick me up. The guys that were helping us looked at us not believing a word we said. We went into the bathroom to confirm our pledge of doing whatever we wanted but not giving up our virginity.

We danced until our legs became sore. We smoked and drank until we both became paranoid. We kept reminding each other of our intent to stay for a little while. A little while turned into 5 am. We got into the car and decided to sleep in the car with the windows cracked for an hour or two because we knew Dexter would not be back until Sunday. This was Saturday morning. We had nothing to worry about at this point.

April and I woke up to see Mark House coming out of a hotel room with our other neighbor Kathy. How could she do this to me? She knew I was in love with him. I got out and screamed out to him, "You dog! I will never talk to you or her again!" He ran over to the car before April could get it started. He kept making his case that I wasn't giving it up but she was and a man would be a man. April took off. We picked up some breakfast and headed to the house.

When April and I arrived back at the house, Dexter's car was there parked in the handicapped space. This was something he did when he was making a quick run or too tired to walk. I knew he was not going to take this lightly. There was no one in town to break us up if we fought. So April and I sat in the car hoping he would leave. After two hours of sitting in the car. April had to get her mom's car home. We'd finally gotten a phone but I was scared to go into the house so she could call her mom. Eventually, we decided to go in to face the wrath. There was no need for us both to get into trouble. So in we went so April could call her mother.

I walked in first. He was livid. This light skinned big man had transformed into a large red tomato. He called me every bitch name under the sun. I sat there with no rebuttal. April was on the phone explaining to her mom why she was late. So in my mind I pictured him as a red tomato talking with no reaction. That pissed him off even more. Then came the words that would forever change my life when he hollered and screamed, "GO PACK YOUR SHIT, YOU HARD HEADED BITCH!!

YOU ARE TAKING YOUR ASS TO GEORGETOWN AND YOU WILL NEVER COME BACK IN MY HOUSE. SEE HOW YOU LIKE LIVING WITH THEM PO ASS NIGGAS!!"I dropped to my knees pleading for him not to separate me from April. He kept insisting that I pack my bags because he was dropping me off at the airport and I would be responsible for getting a ticket and getting to that country ass town. April was crying on the phone with her mom telling her what was going on and repeating, "He is making her leave!" As I continued to beg and plead to stay because I would be starting school that Monday, April handed him the phone. I could hear Mrs. Mooney asking if I could stay with them until things cooled down or until I finished school. He gathered his composure and spoke with such grand articulation. In shock I stopped crying and began to listen. I took a deep breath just in case I would have to talk to Mrs. Mooney. When he was done telling her no, I could not stay with them, he handed me the phone. April was crying so hard. I reassured Mrs. Mooney I would probably be back in a few days when my mother came back so not to worry. I gave April the phone. She told her mother goodbye and hung up the phone. We hugged a little extra and then she left. Dexter only let me pack the essentials. He stressed that I was leaving his home with what I came with and that was N-O-T-H-I-N-G.

He dropped me off in front of the airport. I didn't know how to purchase a ticket. But I figured it out. It was a relief not having to hear his mouth. Knowing that I had a few hours before the flight left, I got some change and headed to the pay phone to call Mrs. Mooney and let them know I was good and hopefully would be back in a couple of days. I called my Aunt Lisa to ask her to pick me up from the airport. I gave her the arrival time. She reassured me she would be there. Before I knew it I was on a Delta flight headed to Georgetown, South Carolina.

Chapter 10
It was for the Best

I arrived in Georgetown remembering how Dexter had refused to allow me to tell my friends goodbye. "You should have done that last night when you were partying," he said. My Aunt Lisa picked me up from the airport. I stayed at her place for a couple of weeks. She was living in subsidized housing due to her divorce and the layoff at her job. She had started rolling a little bit with Dexter and Jackie but she kept the apartment just in case something went down with Dexter and Jackie's game. I would see Jackie when she'd visit Lisa which was once or twice a week. I think she was either stashing dope or money at Lisa's place. I didn't know that for sure because Jackie had become so secretive. If she was stashing money at Lisa's place, Lisa obviously did not have access to it. I could tell because she was always budgeting her unemployment check.

I finally got the nerve to call Smoothe. I knew he had money but it was like asking a complete stranger.

People in Georgetown called him Smootheman but those close to him called him Smoothe. His God given name was Alan Thomas Dean. He was well known in Georgetown because he hustled hard but was quick to give to an underprivileged mother and child. He had a soft spot for the disadvantaged but he was not to be crossed or there would be consequences. He came to get me with one phone call. He rode me around to all the hustling and gambling spots and introduced me to everybody that came near me or him. The common census was, "She looks just like you." That made him smile every time it was said. He asked me what I liked to do. I told him I liked to play basketball. He bought me an entire outfit from shirt to shoes so we could go play. We went to his trailer off in some cut to change his clothes then we went to the center to play basketball. The whole ride he asked me, "Are you sure you can play?" I would respond by either shaking my head yes or quietly saying, "Yeah I'm sure."

When we arrived at the center I ran a game with the boys. I think he was amazed I could play the way I did and still looked like a girl. He began again telling everybody that I was his daughter. Then he would laugh. He picked me up every day that week to go play ball. When he would drop me off he would ask, "Do you need anything. "I would always say no because the first time he dropped me off he gave me $200 and he always took me to eat. So I was fine. I would get out and say, "Thank you." He would say, "You all right." I knew that meant you are welcomed. I enjoyed the time we spent together. He never cursed at me and every time he looked at me he smiled.

My Dad started off spending time with me daily. Then it stopped. I wondered if I'd did something. Before I could figure it out he'd call with a venture for us. One day he picked me up and took me to get reacquainted with my brothers and sisters. It was a little uneasy going to house after house meeting woman and child after woman and child. After the third house it was routine.

So much had changed since I'd left. When I got a ride out to Maylor everything had changed. Nancy and Sandra had left to live with their biological mother in another town. Mona was in Job Corp. Debra was dating a man twice her age. Suzie had gotten married to a man and was into hardcore drugs. Ma sided with Jackie and felt she couldn't condone me disrespecting an adult the way I disrespected Dexter so our relationship was loving but a little distant. I didn't bother to tell her the details of what I had endured. Plus, I could tell she was enjoying the trinkets Jackie's lifestyle afforded her and Pa. But Pa told me that as far as he was concerned, I always had a home there regardless of what I did. I didn't stay though because I did feel more comfortable at Aunt Lisa's. I had more to do there than in Maylor. Plus, I liked hanging with Smoothe because wherever we went, he gave respect and he got respect. I also appreciated the respect he gave me. In his presence I was secure in the fact that I wouldn't be physically or mentally abused.

Chapter 11
I Finally Feel Like a Child

The summer was ending and Jackie wasn't changing her mind concerning me coming back up to Ann Arbor. Besides, she had some work for Lisa up in Michigan. So, Lisa took me to Smoothe and told him I was going to have to stay with him for the school year. He was so happy. He took me to one of his main girls' houses to try it out. She was only a few years older than me. It didn't work. I could feel things could end up the way they were in Michigan. So I called Brenda and Crystal to ask if I could live with one of them during the school year. I knew they were aware of Dexter's antics and hopefully one of them would understand. They said, "Yes."

Crystal came to pick me up. I stayed at her house for about a week. She told me she wasn't going to have me being dependent on anybody. She took me to get my driver's permit then told Smoothe he needed to start working on getting me a car. They knew each other from back in the day before I was born so she didn't mind being straight with him. She listed everything that would be taking place with me. According to Crystal, I wouldn't be living with one of his women because she would hate to kick one of their asses. She advised that she and Brenda would be keeping me because the closest school serviced her area as well as Brenda's. Brenda also had a conversation with him concerning taking me school shopping as well as the money he would pay for support.

Brenda and Crystal made sure I got my driver's license, a car and lectured me on acting like I had some common sense. I finally had a big smile on my face. If that was all I had to do, then I wouldn't have a problem. Brenda took me into her home and nurtured me like I hadn't been since I left Ma and Pa's house. She made sure I had my clothes washed and ironed. She made sure I had breakfast, lunch and dinner. I was startled the first day I went to school. She had a breakfast sandwich on the table for me to eat because she had to be at work prior to me leaving. Is this paradise? My life was changing. Peace was in the plan. I felt human and loved.

I began high school at Riverbend. I made the basketball team and was a starter on varsity. We were the first girl team in the history of the school to play for the state championship. The only upset while attending Riverbend was the counselors told me I would have to be put back a year because I had changed schools so much and failed the classes that I needed. Smoothe was upset. I wasn't though because I was always a grade ahead and if school was going to be the way

it was going then shoot, I'd stay forever.

There was a guy named Ben I'd met at Riverbend and became his girlfriend.

One day, I was picked to participate in the debutante ball. Of course, Ben would

be my escort. Everything and everybody in my life were perfect. Smoothe was so

active in my life he was voted parent of the year in sports. He walked up to

receive his reward with a neck and mouth full of gold. His grin could have blinded

the sun.

Chapter 12
She is Not Who I need

A month into school, Ben and I were playing a basketball game of 21. I won because of my free throws and outside shots. He chased me out of the gym. As I was running out of the door, it swung back and hit my ankle. It was a small cut and it didn't hurt much. I put a Band-Aid on it when we got back to Brenda's. That week in school, I became deathly ill. As I was walking down the hall everything started spinning and I could barely walk because my right leg was in so much pain. I immediately went to the nurse's office. She took my temperature and said it was 103.5. Then I showed her my swollen leg. She then tried to call Smoothe but nobody answered. She asked how she could get in touch with my parents. I explained the situation and gave her Brenda's work number. Brenda came and picked me up and immediately took me to the doctor's office where Smoothe met us. I was immediately admitted to the hospital.

While in the hospital, I constantly thought, "Wow, I am finally happy but now I'm going to die." I had no energy at all mentally or physically. Lisa was back in town so she stayed days and Brenda stayed nights alternating with Ma. I was somewhat in a fog but I heard the doctors asking for my parents. One of the nurses said her mother is in Michigan finishing her chemo treatments and will be here in a few days. In my mind I said to myself, *"She finished her chemo treatments almost a year ago."* The nurse then informed the doctor that my dad came daily but had a phobia of hospitals. He became dizzy and nauseated when he visited.

After a week in the hospital the doctors started discussing amputating my leg with Ma and Brenda if the new antibiotic they were trying failed to work. Ma began anointing and praying over me. She wanted me to recite a scripture I learned as a child. I was so sick I could only mumble it. Ben would visit me as often as he could borrow his mother's car without letting her know what had happened. He felt it was his fault and she would kill him if she found out.

By the next weekend, Jackie came into the hospital room. She was dressed to the nines. I almost didn't recognize her because she looked so good. She came over to the bed. "You feeling better?" she asked. Out of instinct I said, "Yes." I don't think she touched me. She said she was going out to get a drink and she would be back to spend the night. She put her Louis Vuitton night bag in the closet and left. I woke up from a dream at around 2 am. Jackie was there at the hospital loving and doting over me. I looked around and realized it was a dream so I dozed back off. About 30 minutes later, the smell of Crown Royal and perfume awoke me again. Jackie was already lying on the cot with the blanket over her head when she again asked, "You alright?" I didn't reply. What was the point?

The next morning, the doctors came in and told me they were going to take me to surgery and open up my leg to see if the infection would drain. The surgery might prevent me from losing my leg. They asked me if I had an adult that could sign the consent. I pointed over to the cot and said, "That's my mother over there." I called her name as loud as I could to wake her. Then one of the physicians went over to the cot and shook her. She sat up and out came the correct pronunciation of every word and syllable. The physician explained to her what they were going to do. She signed the form and smiled until they left the room. She then turned over, pulled up the cover and went back to sleep.

After I came back from surgery, Brenda, Ma, Lisa and Jackie were sitting in the room. Jackie was still sitting up on the cot with her silk robe over her silk pajamas. Something was so beautiful and classy about her that I couldn't stay disappointed with her for long. The doctor explained that I would be fine because they were able to drain a significant amount of the infection from my leg which would allow the antibiotic to work. Jackie left the hospital that night. I don't remember seeing her anymore while I was hospitalized.

I was discharged a week later on crutches and antibiotics but I was able to get back to my new existence, my school, my home with Brenda, my relationship with Smoothe and my peace of mind.

The week I returned to school, the librarian asked me if I wanted to be in the debutante ball. I didn't know what it was. She explained the preparation and training I would go through; that it would be a formal ball presenting over 70 girls in Georgetown to society. One morning, she called me into her office to let me know one of my cousins Georgia who was a member of her organization, would be my sponsor. I remember seeing her as a child but couldn't recall her until after she introduced herself at practice. A strong boost of self-esteem came with knowing the women of this town thought that much of me.

The night of the ball was the night I truly felt like a princess. I had a floor length white gown that fit me like it was made for me. Every strand of my hair was in place. My makeup was flawless because Lisa came over to Brenda's to do it. Ben escorted me in a black and white tuxedo that made him look like a prince.

Smoothe presented me in a black and white tux and he truly looked like a king. All 10 fingers were covered with gold and diamonds. His wrist was covered with thicker gold and diamonds. He tried to talk the directors into letting him wear his fur coat. They finally convinced him it was against the rules. He followed the rules and walked me out with just his black tux. The song we danced to was *Endless Love.* The escorts began the waltz...then the fathers interrupted and finished the dance. It was spectacular how we danced and enjoyed ourselves. At the end, I noticed everyone was there except for Dexter and Jackie. She told me she was on her way earlier that day. She must have gotten caught up or her plane was late. It was alright though because the ball was spectacular and established bonds between many of us that would never be broken.

When we arrived back at Brenda's I knew Jackie was there because of the rented black Jaguar parked in front. My plans were to change so Ben and I could go eat and then go to the after party. I already knew Jackie had a good excuse for why she didn't make it. She'd be waiting on the couch with one of her magnetic smiles. I opened the door and ran to the kitchen where she was eating. I sat at the table across from her and began telling her about the ball. Ben sat in the living room after speaking to her. But as I talked, she became furious. She cursed while telling me I wouldn't wear my debutante gown out because I didn't pay for it. I didn't want anything to mess this night up so I didn't mention that I'd come to the house to change. Brenda walked in the door and just looked. I think she heard the commotion from outside or could feel the tension. I didn't say another word as I went to go upstairs. I did a motion with my hands for Ben to go to the car. I changed into a dress she'd complimented on the last time she was in town. Then I went into the kitchen and said, "I will see y'all later," to her and Brenda before I turned to leave. Out of my peripheral, I saw her get up and walk behind me. In my mind I was praying she would tell me to have a good night Instead, she hit me in the back. I felt my soul sink into a place I thought I had escaped. "She doesn't know how to stay in a child's place, "she fumed turning to look at Brenda. I went to the door motioned for Ben to go ahead. I didn't have any response to what was happening and went to bed. I talked to God for about 30 minutes telling him how hurt I was but please DO NOT let me cry. The next morning I called Ben and made up some wild story to make him laugh and to make me feel better. Jackie stayed a few days. She even attended church. Then off to her new destination Fort Lauderdale, Florida she went.

Chapter 13
I Don't Want You Anymore

Jackie returned to Fort Lauderdale. She bought a condominium in an upscale community in Davie. Dexter was still living in Michigan. Her cancer had returned. She was scheduled to begin chemo and radiation in a few days after leaving Georgetown. My Aunt Lisa was moving in to help her while she went through the chemo and radiation. Jackie had decided to take all the boys back into her fold. There was little William (Aunt Lisa's son), Tinsley Lane (Pete's little brother), Little Dexter and Pete. Jackie called me daily wanting me to move to Florida. I would always say, "Not now, I'm playing basketball and we are undefeated and if I graduate here at this school, I have a chance to get a scholarship to college." She would respond, "You can play here." Then I would come up with a reason to get off the phone.

She once called to say she had Aunt Lisa decorate a room just for me and she wasn't going to let anybody in it until I moved down there. I wanted to say, "I don't want you or anything that comes along with you." But the pastor constantly preached about honoring your mother and father would increase your days upon the earth and for the first time in a long time I wanted more days. Jackie wasn't as gruff as usual. The phone calls became more frequent and she got to the point where she would cry before hanging up. I started not answering the phone. I would run into the bathroom and pretend to use it so I would not have to talk to her.

I had a been a long day at practice so Brenda and I turned in early. It was about 11 pm. I fell fast asleep when suddenly I felt a slap across my face. I just knew I was dreaming but then I felt another even harder slap. At that point, I jumped up and grabbed Jackie's hand before she could do it again. I screamed loudly, "What did I do?!" Snatching her hand away she hissed, "You won't answer my fucking calls but you will answer this!" Then she slapped me again. I hollered for Brenda. "Tell her I am playing basketball and most of the time I am tired when I get home!" I didn't hear anything from Brenda...not even her usual snoring. So in my head was Brenda was not there. So I begged and pleaded, "Let me finish my basketball Jackie! My grades are good...I promise! As I wrapped my arms around her legs, she kicked me. My chest hurt but I just assumed it was from my heart breaking. She continued to pack my clothes in the black trash bags. I ran into the bathroom so I could see if Brenda was in her room. She was lying there with her back turned to us. So I could tell either she was alright with what was going on or too hurt to help me. I gave up. I turned towards Jackie to ask permission to put on my shoes and clothes. Her eyes looked like she was saying it was fine. So I did. Then she said, "Don't you worry about this bullshit. I'll buy you more. Just go get in the car." As I began to walk down the stairs she threw two trash bags of clothes behind me. I almost fell but I picked them up and walked to the car. There was Ma and Pa. I ran over to the car thinking they are here to save me. I showed Ma my bleeding lip. She looked down then back up and said, "You'll be alright." Pa began crying hysterically repeating over and over again while holding his head, "I'm sick of this shit." Ma ran over to him with the sternest voice I had ever heard come out of her mouth, "Jim you know she is sick and all she wants is Tam with her." Pa said shaking his head, "It don't have to be this way. It's a damn shame...it don't have to be this way." I got into the passenger side because Pa got out and got into the back seat after slamming the door. Ma had already said Jackie had some business to take care of and was flying down later this week. I looked over at the woman I thought was one of God's Angels and asked, "What happened to the times we use to read the Bible and pray for Jackie when she acted like this?" She looked at me with her eyes turning red as if she wanted to cry and offered, "One day you will understand." I turned towards the window as I continued to hear Pa's muffled sniffles and went to sleep.

I couldn't see the future or understand why she had this hold on them. The only thing that came to mind was Ma didn't want to give back the fur coat she wore to church or the new cars she received every two years. I wondered if they could see that Jackie only wanted me to be her maid or caretaker for the friends and family children she collected. I looked at my grandmother and wondered if she knew I cut dope and transported it regularly. Hopefully, not this saintly woman that taught me to read the Bible and pray nightly.

When we arrived at the condo, we were met by Aunt Lisa at the door. She was so excited to show me my room. She was sure to tell me she'd picked the furniture and the color scheme. I thanked her in a flat tone, got my two trash bags and followed her to the room. There I stayed until Pete came in to welcome me home. He said he was glad that I came. In a sly way I let him know it wasn't my decision but I had no choice. But still Pete gave my dark place some light.

It took a couple of days for Smoothe and the coaches to find out Jackie had basically kidnapped me.

That was the phrase all my friends and teammates used. Smoothe called and pleaded with Jackie to let me come back home and finish the season by telling her that the team needed me. Smoothe was the only person that could change her mind once it had been made up. Reluctantly she gave in and sent me back to Georgetown but not without a word of advice. "Don't make me come back for you. "The basketball team went to the State Championship. We lost but the celebrations after patched my wounded heart. I was just glad to be a part of something so great.

I returned to Ft. Lauderdale keeping my end of the bargain but my mind set had changed. I would not participate in anything they could take away from me. I made it through the semester without much conflict with Jackie. I just stayed in my room as much as possible. She gave me her word I could attend April's graduation and possibly stay the summer. I made my reservations for the day after my last exam. Jackie gave me access to an account that had a substantial amount of money. I knew my summer would be a good one.

Chapter 14
Deadly Consequences

April and her mother were waiting when I arrived at Detroit Metropolitan Airport. They were so glad to see me. I felt like I was home. April and I couldn't wait to compare clothes and pick out new ones for our adventures that summer. We were both shocked to discover we had identical pink and black outfits. That assured us that we truly were best friends. We got dressed and went downtown Ann Arbor to hangout. All the fellas were giving us compliments. We knew we were looking good. I put out the word to tell my old flame I was back in town. I knew Mark would get the message whether he was laid up with someone else or not.

April and I continued to prance up and down the block where we would hang out. We even got into her Mom's green station wagon and circled the block a couple times. We decided to take one more stroll before going to the house. To my surprise, a guy walked up to me and kissed me on the lips. It was Mark House and he started tonguing me like he was in love. We had talked on the phone quite frequently but I just figured it was just talk. Little did he know that by this time, he was not the only man who had kissed me this way. I figured there was no reason to tell him that though. We enjoyed each other that summer. He somehow respected the fact that I wanted to wait until marriage. I'm sure he was getting his fair share of loving but it wasn't mine.

April graduated and we had a continuous celebration until something out of the ordinary happened. Dexter called me and asked if April and I would come watch the boys because he had just gotten to Detroit and had to take care of some business. He promised to make it worth my while with offers of money and putting us up in the Renaissance for a couple of days. He even said we could enjoy the July 4th fireworks on the lake. So after confirming with April and her mom we decided to go.

Within 15 minutes, excitement turned to horror when I received a telephone call from Dexter's next door neighbor who was one of his mules. She also watched his house when he was out of town. What Maggie told me brought me to my knees. Crying hysterically she blurted out, "Dexter just got shot by some men in a blue car!!" I said with skepticism, "There's no way...I just talked to him. I am on my way to keep the boys." She replied, "Tam I am not lying. It just happened. The ambulance is on the way." The next question to her was how did you get this number?" With a sigh she said, "I pressed redial." My next question

was, "Where are the boys?" "They are with Zack in the van going to get

something to eat. They didn't see anything." Zack was once a high roller but got

on the product himself and lowered himself to one of Dexter's gofers. He was

always in Big Dex's corner as long as the money was right. So my next thought

was hoping the hit was not arranged by Zack and that he was not taking the

children to kill them as well.

I hung up the phone and immediately called Jackie. She was devastated but

went into General Jackie mode and started giving out directions. I caught my

breath as she told me what to do. I told April what had taken place. Jackie said I

had to somehow get up to Detroit and make sure the boys were alright even if I

had to catch a cab. The phone rang again. It was Jackie telling me to just get to

Valencia Burns' place in Bellville so she could get to the hospital and keep the

children until she could get a flight. Valencia was an educated woman who held a

Master's degree in Social Work; however she ran hard with the hustlers. She also

had a young son by Desmond that I adored. Desmond was dead by this time from

a mysterious strain of pneumonia. Big Dex refused to visit his only brother when

he was notified he was dying because Desmond did not pay him back the last

$100 he'd let him borrow. They could be such a heartless family. Jackie also said

Brenda was coming from Georgetown and one of them would be there before the

night was over. She was talking to me as if she was in control but I could hear her

crying before she could completely hang up the phone.

Mrs. Mooney reluctantly agreed to take me to Valencia's home. I convinced

her I would be alright. I told her that Valencia was my mother's sister-in-law. I

didn't want them to get involved in this craziness because Mrs. Mooney didn't

know that my parents were in such a sinister business. I needed them to be my

friends and to remain safe.

Once Valencia and I got to the boys they were playing in the park up the

street from Dex's place. That was a way to keep them from knowing what

happened. It was such a relief to see they were safe. I picked up the kids and

drove the van following Valencia in her white Corvette. We arrived at the hospital

and went up to the emergency room floor. The physicians asked if I was the next

of kin. I didn't know what that meant so I said, "No." I just knew Jackie would be

there by 10 or 10:30 and I needed to keep the boys safe and fed. Valencia told

them she was his sister. She would talk to the doctors and come back to me with

the news. "He's been shot seven times with an automatic rifle and they don't think he's going to make it." I immediately fell to my knees and started praying to God. "Please!" I begged. "I take it back... he doesn't have to die. I will be alright. I don't see him much anymore. He's much nicer than he was." Valencia said, "The only thing that is saving his life right now is the fact he is such a large man."

Jackie arrived as she promised but was totally disheveled. I was glad to see Brenda at her side. Jackie was screaming, "My husband, my husband!" I tried to hug her but she didn't want me to touch her. She grabbed up Little Dex and asked him if he was OK. The other children were left with not a word. As I lay in Brenda's arms trying to find some peace and comfort, Jackie came to me questioning me about what the doctors had said. Valencia interrupted and started telling her. She then looked at me as if she didn't trust what Valencia said and asked me, "Is that all?" I nodded my head yes.

The nurses came and took Jackie into a private conference room. She came back out and announced it was going to be a long night and asked Brenda if she would get the kids to a hotel. I gave Brenda the keys and we loaded up the extended Chrysler van and headed for the nearest hotel. We got two adjoining rooms. The boys slept in one room and Brenda and I slept in the other. The next morning, Dexter was out of surgery. They held him in intensive care. The doctors said they had to leave one of the bullets in him because it was too dangerous trying to get it out.

The boys and I stayed at the room so as not to get on anybody's nerves. We finally got permission to go to the hospital on the third day since Smoothe was flying up to get me. He felt too much was going on for me to stay there. Jackie said he was going to bring someone with him so they could take the children back as well. When I walked into Dexter's room, I saw he had a machine breathing for him. But he was able to write notes. I was smiling but tears ran down my face. I wanted to do a full blown cry but Jackie instructed me not to go in there with all that emotion because he didn't need that right now. I walked up to the bed and laid my head on him. He nudged me a little. Then he wrote me a note that read, *Get out of my room.* I showed it to Brenda. She said it was the medicine talking. I immediately went to the pay phone, used my prepaid card and called April. I needed to know something. "Do you think he somehow knows I wanted him dead for the way he treated me?" She readily assured me, "There's no way he would. Plus you took it back." A number of hustlers were summoned by Jackie with one phone call. She told them to bring the heavy artillery. The ICU waiting room was packed. I never went back into his room.

Dexter survived 13 days. Then we received the phone call that someone had pulled the tube out and he was dead. I could hear Jackie on the telephone explaining to Aunt Lisa, "I trusted these muthafucka's at this hospital," she fumed. "They let somebody in here to kill him. Last night, they told us we needed to leave the lobby because we were too noisy and it was bothering the other patients. They assured me they would have a security guard on watch. He was having the surgery to pull that breathing tube out and get a tracheostomy so he could breathe on his own and somebody went in there and pulled it out. They are going to have Hell to pay." The next words out of Aunt Lisa's mouth were, "We are on our way."

Jackie was furious that no one owned up to the hit. But she was determined to find out who was responsible. So she sent a team out on the streets. She would come to my room because she had it designated as the safe room. I was on a different floor and in a different wing. My room was where she discussed her top secret plans regarding things that occurred. Raheim was the only person who knew where I was because he was the only person she fully trusted at this time. By the conversations they would have, I knew a lot of people were dying. She brought a guy into my room I didn't know that started talking immediately when he entered, "Some of these shootings that they are reporting on the news aren't ours." Then he started laughing. I just looked up and held my breath. Next I heard Jackie say she got word on the street that Valencia was in cahoots with the people who killed Dexter because she had a big insurance policy on him. Valencia was known for insurance fraud. Before I knew it, I jumped up and screamed out, "No! She is our friend!" Jackie responded to my outburst by saying, "If you want that baby of hers to live then you best take care of him when he is handed to you." Then she got up and walked out. Raheim and the strange man followed.

The next morning, Jackie brought me Valencia's baby boy. She said Valencia has class and wants you to watch him. This was not abnormal because I would keep the baby often when she went to class. I was praying that she was telling me the truth. She gave me money to go get some food, Pampers and milk. Then she left. Valencia was a doting mother. But I knew my suspicions were confirmed that they'd killed her when she didn't come for the baby after two days.

Raheim brought these two women to my room and introduced them as Valencia's sisters. "They came to get the baby," he said. I looked at the sisters and asked, "Where is Valencia?" They both looked at me with an angry disposition.

Then the older sister said," She's dead...they found her on the side of the road."

The tears raced down my face as they took the baby without saying another

word. For the first time ever, I really wanted my daddy. So I called him. I gave him

Jackie's room number so he could call her. First he called her then called me back.

He said, "I will be there on the next flight." He arrived around midnight. That was

one pick up from the airport I was glad to do. We went to the hotel and directly to

Jackie's room. His girlfriend and I sat on the bed closest to the door. I heard him

tell Jackie to take her husband home and give him a proper burial. Her priority

was getting her family out of the line of fire. He guaranteed that he would stay

back and take care of what she needed done in Detroit. For the first time I saw

weakness in Jackie. She started to walk away. Smoothe grabbed her arm...pulled

her close to him and held her while she cried like a baby for the first time since

Dexter's death.

The next day, we all were scheduled to fly out to Georgetown. The ones

that weren't flying drove. As we walked through the airport ready to go to our

gates, we were surrounded by plain clothes police. They herded us up like cattle

and took us downstairs to the airport jail. I would have never imagined there was

a jail in the airport. They didn't search anyone. They just had questions they wanted to ask concerning Dexter and Valencia's death. I was a minor so I was placed in a seat near the door. I think I had a couple of ounces of cocaine and something strapped to my back.

The cops said they were going to transport us to the main jail. Jackie looked at me and mouthed get rid of it while she let out a screaming cry to distract the police. I quietly asked one of them if I could go to the restroom. They let me go but stood outside the door. First, I looked for cameras. Then I flushed what was in my pockets. I had a time getting the stuff off that was taped to my back. I did it but my skin was irritated and raw. I had to empty that one first then in went the bags as well. Finally, it was all gone as well as the stomach pains I had due to nervousness. When I walked back into the room, I held my palms up indicating to anyone that knew our game that all was clear. After we were interrogated, we were allowed to leave the next day. The police put us up in a hotel and reimbursed us for the airline tickets.

Chapter 15
Hold on a Little While Longer

The funeral was a dramatic event. I screamed the entire time. I felt it was my fault. I remembered praying so hard for Dexter to die. Listing them one by one in the order I wanted them to die, he was first on my list. There was a party after the funeral. It was called a repast. It consisted of food, drinking and dancing. The fellowship was made up of hustlers from all over dressed in what they're part of the country deemed sharp. I didn't understand why Smoothe, Jackie, Raheim and I sat at the same table. I later found out it was a form of protection because they didn't know where the hit came from. The love expressed in the condolences seemed so genuine but the conversation at the table disputed every hug and kiss. Jackie was constantly analyzing the mannerisms to see if she discerned any guilt while seeking opinions from Smoothe and Raheim. "Please don't let anybody else die...at least not tonight," I prayed.

A few days later, we drove back to Ft. Lauderdale. My stomach ached from guilt. Wishing death on someone was not the Christian thing to do. I couldn't share this with anyone but April. She reassured me I had no control over life and death so I need to forgive myself. As we road back home Jackie said we'd never have to worry about finances. She'd just received a check from the insurance company for a $100,000. "Once I make a few turnovers we want have to worry at all," she promised. "First thing I'm going to buy is a house...cash." It seemed like a calmness came over everybody in the yellow van. But it was taken back when she said "I'm starting back on chemo Monday." I didn't have a comment. I had become familiar with the chemo and the cancer. I really didn't care how anyone else felt at this time. I tucked my pillow under my head and fell asleep until it was my turn to drive.

This was the first time we had no men in the home. It was just the women and the children. Smoothe would occasionally come down driving his Mercedes-Benz. When he'd visit, he and Jackie would disappear while I entertained his new young girlfriends. Smooth and Jackie would be gone for hours. Then they would come back with jewelry from the flea market, clothes from some high end store and a connection I didn't know how to explain. The young girls he would bring would be no more than two to maybe four years older than me. Most of the time, we would have a lot in common so we would easily bond.

Finally, it was my senior year. I was so excited! This was the first time I had been at a school continuously for a year and a half I enjoyed my senior year. I hung out with a middle class crew. But I never felt I belonged. Because I lived in Jacaranda, my friends felt I was upper middle class. I never told what went on in my home. They would never understand. There was a guy I met named Walter who was somewhat of a bully at school. He'd ask for a dollar from every one that passed him in the hall. "Hey Baby Girl...let me hold a dollar," he said to me as I walked to class one day. "What do you need it for?" I asked. He responded with a smile that was almost perfect except for the chipped tooth in front. He was very muscular with a Florida black tan. Something was so familiar about him. He had a protector's spirit. Mona, one of the girls I'd met the year before, grabbed me by the arm and pulled me away. "He's trash," she whispered in my ear and escorted me to class giving me his history of being homeless. She also informed me that his mother was on drugs. Little did she know that made him more attractive to me. I loved the underdog because I was one.

The next day he came up to me asking for a dollar. I gave him $20. He reached in his pocket and gave me 19 dollars. I said, "No! I'm giving you the whole twenty." He wouldn't take it. I put the ones in my pocket and walked off. He ran up behind me and grabbed me by the waist and asked "Where are you from?" I said "South Carolina." Regardless of all the warnings I'd been given, I felt so protected by him. I didn't care if sometimes I had to feed him or give him money to get his lights turned back on. I knew his story and he knew mine.

It was prom time and Walter was my date. He was even more excited than me when he found out Smoothe had ordered us a limo and it was going to pick him up first. He jumped up and down. I could tell he wanted to cry but he held it. He asked over and over again, "Are you sure they will pick me up at my house?" He asked, "I can walk up to the school. It won't be a problem." Walter was insecure because he lived deep in the hood with his older brother in a cement building with no air conditioning or heat. Fans were the best they could do for comfort. Trash was lined up from the beginning of his building up to the entrance of his door. Liquor bottles dominated the parking spaces and the phone booth which belonged to everybody that lived in this pink cement hell hole. I felt like a princess every time I pulled up. They never offered me drugs and my car was never vandalized because I was Walter's girl.

I was getting ready for the prom and wondered where Jackie was? No one was home. I was worried that something was getting ready to happen. "Oh Lord,

I'm going to have to do this without a mother," I thought. I called Aunt Lisa's job at American Express. She answered and said she was on her way. I needed someone to help me with my makeup. The limo would be here soon. Aunt Lisa arrived as promised and started making up my face. In walked Jackie. I started to cry. She walked up to me...pushed my head and said, "Shut the fuck up! You don't appreciate anything. I'm out making fucking money and here you are here crying about a prom." She then turned around and went to her room. Aunt Lisa just patted my face with a Kleenex. She then looked me deeply in my eyes and said, "DON'T...LET...HIM...FUCK..YOU." Shoot, Walter and I had not gone *that* far with almost a year under our belt. He understood that it was something I was determined to hold onto. But I'm sure his baby mama met that need.

The limo finally pulled up. Walter got out. He looked like a movie star. The neighbors watched him escort me to my chariot. My Aunt Lisa took pictures as I got into the car. Walter asked, "Why are you crying? Are you that happy? I just said, "Yes." We enjoyed the night. It made me so happy to know this was an experience Walter would never stop smiling about.

Graduation finally arrived and at least 15 people came to see me walk across the stage including Smoothe and a girl who had made at least three trips to

Florida with him. I remember her name was Marge. My grandmothers, my grandfather, Aunt Lisa and my girl April were there as well. Smoothe and Jackie had also invited a bunch of their friends. I didn't have the heart to tell them I only had four tickets. So I decided to let the whole thing play out.

It was time for me to be at the auditorium but nobody was ready to leave but Smoothe, Marge, April and myself. I was so tired. I really didn't care if anybody else came or was able to get into the graduation. But I did want Brenda to come. But I also knew that if I chose her over Jackie...whew! The fallout would have been epic. At either rate, I did it. I walked across that stage and received my diploma. My grade point average was 1.9 but I made it!

After graduation, Smoothe and I didn't see any of the people that was a part of my graduating party but I did see Walter. I was proud of him and he was proud of me too. We made plans to meet up later. He was going to show his diploma to his mom and dad. The only one who made it to the graduation was his brother Gregory.

It was around 11 pm. when we finally caught up with Jackie and the other people who came to attend the graduation. The animosity was thick when we walked into the house. I expected an explosion from Jackie. But the only thing she said was, "All these people wanted to see you graduate and we couldn't even get into the place." I looked surprised because I was expecting to get slapped but she just turned around and walked up the stairs to her room. People in the room gave me my congratulations but I could tell it was coming from a dry place. I deserved it though so it was OK. April and I went upstairs to dress and then went to meet Walter and his friends. While she was uncomfortable with Walter and his friends she'd do anything for our friendship.

My dream was to enroll in Tuskegee with April to join their nursing program. However, Jackie had a temper tantrum when I asked her a question that I needed to answer for the school's application. When she flatly stated, "You won't be going to that nigger school." I knew then the battle was not worth fighting. So April and I sat down and figured we would discuss it with her mom who suggested that I go to a community college in the area. I went and registered at Broward. Our hope was maybe Jackie would change her mind by the next semester. After the talk about Tuskegee, Jackie wanted to send April home. She had a job she needed me to do. The job included a ride to Georgia and April would just be in the way, Jackie concluded. We begged anyway and suggested that April could help drive since we only had two more weeks together. It just so happened, Raheim had stopped by for a day and somehow talked Jackie into letting her ride with us. Later on that year, we would find that Raheim had stolen April's identity.

We enjoyed our trip to Georgia. April and I basically stayed in a hotel and hung out at the mall while people picked Jackie up and dropped her off. She didn't share with me what was going on and I really didn't want to know. My main concern was relishing the last few days of friendship and laughter I'd have with my best friend. April and I would have until next summer to hang out again.

Chapter 16
She is not as Strong as Everyone Thinks

The semester following high school graduation, I entered Broward Community College. April instructed me on how to get financial aid since Jackie was on disability. She told me I would be sure to get it.

All of a sudden, Jackie started losing her hair. She never lost her hair regardless of the chemotherapy she took. But she'd gotten to the point where she was so weak, she couldn't tolerate the kids. So she sent some of the boys home. The only kids she kept were Dexter III because he was hers and William stayed because he was Aunt Lisa's and they lived with us. Pete, who was now 13 also stayed because he helped around the house.

Out of nowhere, Jackie started rambling with her speech and making impulsive decisions. I was now in charge of all household financial decisions including paying the mortgage, light bill and phone bill.

We moved into the house in Pineville, Florida that she'd always promised. It had five bedrooms and an indoor pool. The backyard had orange trees. The neighbors had lemon trees. Never had I seen such citrus fruit growing from trees.

I was from South Carolina where we had apple, pear and peach trees. This was one time Jackie kept her promise.

Then I noticed she began to cry a lot. I knew she cared for Dexter but never thought she loved him enough to cry every time the day he died came around. So on the 20th of every month, she would break down. She would close the door and it would be just me and her. She would cry and throw things stating, "You don't know how I feel!" I would always reassure her that it was going to be OK. She seemed to hold it together for the rest of the month. She had this one boyfriend who she had prior to Dexter's death. He'd come one or two times a month. He couldn't come more often than that though because he was a married man.

One month she was crying more than usual. Papers were all over the place. She showed me her insurance policy. "I thought I was leaving y'all a $100,000 policy when I die...but this is an accidental death policy," she said dryly. "Are you dying?" I asked. She said she wasn't so I took her at her word. Still, something didn't sit well with her answer. I continued to listen. She whimpered "I tried to make a move with this new guy but he just disappeared with $45,000." I tried to reassure her that he might return. "I haven't heard from that muthafucka in a month!" she replied. The more I tried to comfort her the angrier she became. My thoughts were in another place though. I was wondering if she was dying. Looking

at her I could clearly see she was half the woman she was just months ago.

Radiation covered her entire left side. She walked with a cane. She used oxygen.

Anytime she would fly she would use a wheelchair. I knew for a fact she was a

strong woman. She had defeated cancer twice and she would do it again. Still I

planned to go to Dr. Abrams' office and ask him myself.

The following Monday morning I went to the Doctor's office. I went up to

the desk and was so direct it stunned the person behind the desk when I asked "Is

my mother dying?" The nurse looked at me from behind her glasses. "Who is your

mother?" she asked. "You know me," I said. "I bring my mother over here all the

time...Jackie Clinkscale." The nurse stared for a second or two and then said,

"Hold on...I'll be right back." It took at least 20 minutes for her to return. When

she finally came back to the desk, her eyes were red as if she had been crying. I

noticed she wasn't wearing her glasses but she told me that Jackie wasn't dying.

That was all I needed to hear.

Chapter 17
Her Last Breath

It was the end of my second semester. I stayed at Broward because Walter and I had become intimate. I was in love did not want to leave him. I felt marriage and a normal family was on the way. Walter and I both deserved that much in this life. I was so encouraged. The atmosphere in our home was calmer. Jackie and I didn't have to make any runs because now people were coming to us. She explained that we weren't making as much money but we could survive. I took that to mean once Jackie felt better the games would begin again.

One day Jackie had problems breathing so Aunt Lisa took her back to the hospital. I expected her to go in for a couple of days and come back home. But I came home to an empty house. I needed to tell someone I had a 3.7 GPA and would be admitted to the nursing program. The phone rang so I answered. The lady on the other on the other end introduced herself as the nurse who was taking care of Jackie Clinkscale. She asked if I was her daughter. I told her I was. She told me I needed to get over to the hospital. I asked her why. She simply said, "Your mother is dying." I dropped to the floor. I didn't know what to do. But I picked the phone back up and told her I was on my way. I went directly to the school. I knew Walter was there in his English class. It was completely dark when I entered Mrs. Crain's room. She had been my teacher the previous semester. "Mrs. Crain," I said weakly. "I'm looking for Walter Oliver. I got a call from the hospital that my mother is dying." The teacher quietly dismissed her class while I sobbed in a corner. She came over to me and said, "Sweetheart, Walter is not in class today...but I will take you. You don't need to be driving." This five-foot woman with natural unkempt hair, held all of my being in her hands. She gathered her papers, walked me to her car and off we went to the hospital.

She offered me prayer before we went up to my mother's room. It gave me a sense of peace. I was wracked with anxiety from wanting to see what was actually going on with Jackie.

When I entered the room, Jackie was panting with an oxygen mask covering most of her face. I grabbed her shoulders to make sure she could see my eyes and said, "Jackie they said you are dying." She rubbed my head as she said, "No I'm not." She forced the next breath inside her lungs. "They gave me too much medicine," she said as she stretched her eyes looking for the next breath. Mrs. Crain offered to pray with Jackie. She reached out her hands and accepted it.

Dr. Abrams came into the room. He asked to see me in the hall. Without much emotion he said, "Your mother is dying and you need to make a decision as

112

to whether or not we should code her if her heart stops and she stops breathing." He could tell I was confused. So he gently expressed, "If your mom stops breathing...you have to make a decision. Should we bang on her chest to bring her back and put her on a ventilator? Because if we do...she will never be your mother again... or we can just let her go peacefully." My first response was to ask him to give her some more chemo. He quietly said, "It won't help. Her cancer is in her lungs, bones, liver, brain and her eyes. She hasn't seen you guys clearly in months." I was dumbstruck. "She didn't tell us that," I said still in disbelief. "She said you guys gave her too much medicine." Dr. Abrams let out a sigh and said, "We did a bronchoscope to look down into her lungs. She didn't get too much medicine."

I told him I would have to contact some people. I called Brenda who said she was on her way. Then I called Grandma Mary. She'd just left the hospital herself because her mama had just died. How much more were we going to have to go through in one day? I also called Aunt Lisa at her job. She would come as soon as possible but the decision still had to be made. And I had to make it.

Chapter 18
I Knew Him and So Did She

Jackie's parents and other family members stayed at the hospital through the next few nights. I was criticized for it but the fear that percolated in my stomach wouldn't allow me to stay past sundown. So I didn't. I constantly had to explain to people why I didn't want to stay with my mother in her last hours. When the questioning became overbearing I started crying and asked Walter to take me home. I felt guilty that none of my emotions were genuine. Who was I becoming?

It took three weeks but the call finally came. It was Ma. "She's taking her last breaths so you and the boys need to get over here." I could tell she was choking back tears. Walter was there with me. I felt so protected. I didn't feel broken. I called Smoothe to convey the message. "Alright," he said. Then we hung up. It was unusual to me that he didn't come down once since we were told she was dying. Why wasn't he here?

When I entered the room, Jackie lay there lifeless. A sheet covered her body. She was so yellow! Her hair was short with a natural curl. All I could do was touch her. I had done enough crying. At this point, nobody could make me cry so I began comforting others. I especially grabbed a tight grip on Dexter III. I could tell he didn't know what to do. I could only reassure him by saying, "You and I are together forever."

On the ride back home to Pineville, I shared with Walter that my period was three weeks late. He insisted this was not the time to talk about it. I immediately saw in his eyes that he was not the man I thought he would be. I began with, "I think being pregnant would be the best birthday present ever... especially by the first man I ever been with intimately."

He gave me a look that instantly broke my soul. His eyes turned so red. He looked straight as he drove. After a few minutes of uncomfortable silence, he announced, "I...DON'T...WANT...ANY...MORE... CHILDREN!! You know I'm in school trying to make a better life for myself." My eyes filled with water. Everything in me ached. This hurt worse than seeing the woman who birthed me lying there lifeless. I screamed in octaves I didn't know I had. "You said you loved me and we were going to get married!!" He replied wiping sweat from his brow. "I care for you and maybe even love you...but my counselor said I have a chance to make something of myself!" he replied. "All I need to do is not get on drugs; not have any more children; get my associate's degree then enter the military. I don't want to live like I live now. I want my mama and daddy to be proud of me. I'm 18 years old! You will be 18 in a few days. We have forever to have babies." That sounded so familiar. I remembered these words coming from April's mama and my grandmother.

Just like that...my protector had just become my rejecter. I reminded him that he said he never loved his baby mama but allowed her to carry his seed. But now me, the woman who he said he loved wouldn't get that chance. He shook from the tears that were now flowing down his cheeks. But just as he wept, I sucked in my emotions, put a smile on my face and helped him wipe his tears. When we arrived in front of my house I got out the car told him I wish him the best in life. He reached out to hug me but I pushed him back and walked into the house carrying nothing but remorse and the thought of death. I cried myself to sleep that night. I was so overwhelmed. No one thing outweighed the other...it was just pain.

The next morning, I felt a little better. I had to keep pushing. That was one of the phrases Jackie used. Everybody else drove to Georgetown. I had to board the plane with my mother's corpse in the bottom of it. I was leaving behind a man with whom I shared false security and the most pure and intimate part of myself. In the air looking through the clouds I was saying to myself, *"We will bury her on my birthday."* Is there an angel that knows my name?

Chapter 19
I Got to Get Home

"Tammy, what's wrong with you tonight? "Barbara, one of the charge nurses laughingly asked. "You have been quiet all night. Are you sure you are OK? Did those two codes back to back get to you?" I looked at her wanting to say, "Nah...just a screwed up past but right now is reimbursement for it." Instead, I smiled ever so gently and said, "I am going to have to pass up coffee this morning. You know I have to get the boys packed for our Miami vacation. We leave tomorrow morning."

I gave the oncoming nurses a report on their patients. Each of them asked me if I was OK. "Just need to get home in a hurry," I'd reply with a fake smile and a wink. When I'd finished giving reports, I packed my stethoscope in my nursing bag, moved as quickly as I could to the elevator and pressed down. Once those doors opened a little sigh of relief came over me because the anxiety of getting home was lessening.

As I got into my black Volvo Xc90, I put in one of my favorite inspiration tapes, turned the volume up as high as it would go and pulled my hair out of the bun on top of my head. Then I put on my favorite pair of sunglasses and let down every window. It didn't matter to me that it was 45 degrees. I casually put on my red MAC lipstick and headed to my place of peace. I was going to ride hard with my hair blowing in the wind.

As I drove, I began listing mentally and verbally the things for which I was grateful as loud as I could. I began with being grateful for having a God that would never forsake me regardless of what the situation looked like. I was grateful for having my right mind, good health as well as a husband that loves God and me. I was thankful that my husband was a provider and protector. I was thankful to be blessed to have such beautiful and healthy children...blessed to be an educated woman who is doing a job she loves. I'm blessed to have a peaceful home, reliable transportation, faithful friends and family, last but not least I'm blessed to have faith in knowing that God is always there in the midnight hour.

Just one caring relationship early in life gives any child a much better shot at growing up healthy.

-Jack Shonkoff

Made in the USA
Middletown, DE
14 March 2022

62579791R00070